Positively

Also by Courtney Sheinmel

My So-Called Family

Courtney Sheinmel

Positively

Simon & Schuster Books for Young Readers
New York   London   Toronto   Sydney

The author is donating a portion of her proceeds
from this book to the Elizabeth Glaser
Pediatric AIDS Foundation.

SIMON & SCHUSTER BOOKS FOR YOUNG READERS
An imprint of Simon & Schuster Children's Publishing Division
1230 Avenue of the Americas, New York, New York 10020

SIMON & SCHUSTER BOOKS FOR YOUNG READERS is a trademark of Simon & Schuster, Inc.
For information about special discounts for bulk purchases, please contact Simon & Schuster
Special Sales at 1-866-506-1949 or business@simonandschuster.com.
The Simon & Schuster Speakers Bureau can bring authors to your live event. For more
information or to book an event, contact the Simon & Schuster Speakers Bureau at
1-866-248-3049 or visit our website at www.simonspeakers.com.
Book design by Krista Vossen
The text for this book is set in Fournier MT Std.
Manufactured in the United States of America
2 4 6 8 10 9 7 5 3 1
Library of Congress Cataloging-in-Publication Data
Sheinmel, Courtney.
Positively / Courtney Sheinmel.—1st ed.
p. cm.
Summary: Thirteen-year-old Emmy, grieving over her mother who died of AIDS, resentful
of having to live with her father and pregnant stepmother, and despairing about her future,
finds hope at a summer camp for HIV-positive girls like herself. Includes facts about Elizabeth
Glaser, one of the founders of the Pediatric AIDS Foundation.
ISBN 978-1-4169-7169-6
ISBN 978-1-4169-9677-4 (eBook)
[1. HIV (Viruses)—Fiction. 2. AIDS (Disease)—Fiction. 3. Despair—Fiction.
4. Death—Fiction. 5. Grief—Fiction. 6. Stepfamilies—Fiction. 7. Camps—Fiction.
8. Friendship—Fiction.] I. Title.
PZ7.S54124Pos 2009
[Fic]—dc22
2008035447

FIRST
EDITION

For Arielle,
my honorable &
fashionable best friend

• Acknowledgments •

My love and gratitude to my parents, Elaine Sheinmel and Joel Sheinmel, who always told me I would grow up to be a writer . . . and kept believing it even after I went to law school. I am also indebted to my extended family, both real and faux, for boundless support and great company, especially to Phil Getter (a.k.a. Faux Pa) for delicious dinners whenever I needed refueling; and to my friends for being incredibly understanding all the times that I cancelled plans or didn't read the book for book club while I was writing this book. I hope I produced something that makes you proud.

Thank you to Susie Zeegen, Susan DeLaurentis, and the entire staff of the Elizabeth Glaser Pediatric AIDS Foundation, both past and present, for always welcoming me into the office and at Foundation events; to Pam Barnes, Uma Mehta, and Leigh Oblinger for their incredible support of *Positively*; and to Samantha Anobile, who opened her home in Los Angeles to me when I needed a place to stay. My thanks as well to my friends who have donated their time and money to the Foundation over the years, especially Amy Bressler & Eric Shuffler, Maria Crocitto, Jennifer Daly, Courtney Fleischman, Morgan Fleischman, Jennie Rosenberg, and my sister, Alyssa Sheinmel. Special thanks to my best friend Arielle Warshall Katz, who has traveled thousands of miles to support the Foundation (and me). I am also enormously grateful to Jake Glaser for his continued friendship and belief in my books.

Thank you to my agent, Alex Glass, who encouraged me to write this story; and to my editor, David Gale, who believed in it from the first few chapters. Thanks to everyone at Trident Media Group—especially Lara Allen, Adam Friedstein, and Dan Harvey. And thank you to the incredible team at Simon & Schuster—especially Justin Chanda, Paul Crichton, Katrina Groover, Molly McLeod, Nicole Russo, Krista Vossen, Chava Wolin, and the amazing Navah Wolfe.

My deepest thanks to Carol DiPaolo, without whom I wouldn't have been able to write this book; to Kristen H. and her sisters, who patiently answered all of my questions; and to Mandi Swan, for her generous evaluation of the manuscript.

Heartfelt thanks to my incredible, tireless readers—Marachel and Lily Leib, who read the first couple of chapters and told me it was something they wanted to see more of; Lindsay Aaronson, Amanda Berlin, Jackie Friedland, and Llen Pomeroy, who kept reading as I wrote; Laura Liss, who read quickly when I needed her advice; and Nicki Liss, the very first person to put *Positively* on her Facebook list of favorite books. And thanks, as always, to Mary Gordon.

And, finally, my unending appreciation and admiration to Elizabeth Glaser, for inspiration far beyond the pages of this book.

What is yours you'll never lose, and what's ahead may shine.

—SHERYL CROW

Chapter 1

When my mother died I imagined God was thinking, "One down, and one to go."

We were an ordinary family up until Mom got sick. I don't really remember what it was like to be ordinary, since I was only four years old when it all changed. Most of my life I've been different from everybody else.

But sometimes I look at the pictures of us from before. A regular family. A mom, a dad, a little girl. I can tell when Mom was getting sick by how old I look in the pictures, and whether or not I have bangs. The first time Mom got really sick was right around the time I started to grow out my bangs, so my favorite pictures are the ones where I still have bangs and I know for sure that she was healthy. When my bangs are too long and clipped back from my forehead, I know that means Mom is closer to dying.

I don't remember the first time Mom told me she was sick, and that I could get sick too. It seems like something I've always known. At first, Mom just had a cold. It wasn't a big deal, because people get colds all the time, even though Mom was the kind of person who never got sick. But I was in preschool, so she thought maybe I'd brought home germs from the other kids and given them to her. She figured it was just a normal cold like regular people get. Except Mom's cold just wouldn't go away. She went to the doctor and he put her on antibiotics and said it should clear up in a few days, but Mom got worse. One night she couldn't breathe at all, and Dad rushed her to the hospital. It turned out she had pneumonia, but it was more than that. The doctors at the hospital said the reason Mom had pneumonia was because she also had a disease called AIDS. They said Dad and I also had to be tested to see if we were infected with it too. Dad wasn't, but I was. They figured out that Mom had gotten infected before I was born, and I got it when she was pregnant with me.

Mom went on special medication for people with AIDS, and she got better for a while. Even though I wasn't sick, the doctors said I could get sick at any time because I was HIV-positive, which means the virus that causes AIDS is in my blood. From then on, Mom and I had to go to the doctor every couple of months. They tested our blood for things called viral loads and T-cells. If our viral loads were high and our T-cell levels were low, it meant we could be really sick. My blood was drawn so many times I wondered if I would eventually run out. Every time Mom or I got a cold or a stomachache, we had to go to the doctor to make sure it wasn't something worse. After a while, I started having to take the medication too. Sometimes Mom would look at me and start to cry, but usually she pretended she wasn't crying. She would say something dumb, like there was something in her eye or she was remembering a sad movie.

The last thing Mom said to me was "I love you to the sky." It was this game we used to play from when I was little. "Do you love me to the top of my head?" I'd ask. "Higher," Mom would say. "Do you love me to the top of that tree?" "Even higher." "Do you love me to the roof?" "Higher than that." "How high do you love me?" I'd finally ask, and Mom would say, "I love you to the sky."

She died on a Tuesday morning. Afterward the men from the funeral home came to take her body away, and Mom's friend Lisa took me outside. It was too hard to breathe in the house, but the air outside was cool and crisp. It was April, and we sat on the lawn in front of the house. I bent my legs and rested my chin on top of my knees. It had happened way too fast. She was coughing and coughing for months, but she didn't seem that sick. And then all of a sudden she was really sick. My parents had divorced when I was eight years old, so my dad didn't live with us anymore. When Mom got too sick for us to live on our own, different people came to stay. Mom's father came up to Connecticut from Florida; then her sister, my aunt Laura, came in from Colorado. The last two weeks Lisa had come. And we had nurses in and out of the house. But I still didn't really believe that Mom would actually ever die. Even after it happened, I wasn't sure I believed it. I always thought that we would be all right, just because I couldn't imagine it any other way.

Lisa put her hand on my head. I had known her my whole life. She and my mother were best friends from college. I pretended it was Mom's fingers running though my hair. Lisa was pulling at a knot in my hair and my mother was dead. I could hear the ordinary, everyday sounds—wheels against pavement, wind rustling the leaves in the trees. A car drove by, like it was any other day. Why was everything still moving? I felt like everything should have stopped. How was I still breathing? I sucked in my breath and held it to see if it was possible to make time stop, but I could still feel my heart beating in my chest and I let my breath out slowly.

"What can I do, Emmy?" Lisa asked.

I didn't answer. *Mommy,* I said to myself silently, matching up the word to the beats in my chest. *Mom-my, Mom-my, Mom-my.* I said it over and over again in my head, like I was calling out to her. *Mommy.* It was a weird word. It was two words put together, like a compound word: "Mom" and "me." As if we were connected, even though there wouldn't ever be a mom and me again.

I thought about who I was right then, on the last day I had a mother. I had just turned thirteen. I was finishing up seventh grade. I was on the short side; my hair was just past my shoulders. That was how she knew me. The problem is, when someone dies, you keep growing. Things about me would change and she wouldn't be there to see them.

And what if I forgot things about her? My grandmother had died when I was nine, and there were things about her I couldn't remember. Like her voice. I couldn't remember anything about it, not even how she sounded when she said my name.

Sitting on the grass with Lisa, I could still hear Mom's voice in my head. I closed my eyes and could hear her saying my name. I decided to practice remembering it every day so I wouldn't ever forget it.

"Emmy," Lisa said, and I opened my eyes. "I spoke to your father. He said he wants to come over, but I told him I needed to ask you."

I thought of my father driving up our block in his white sedan and pulling into the driveway behind Mom's red car. "No," I said. "I don't want him to come here."

It didn't seem right for Dad to be at Mom's house. After all, he had divorced Mom. He had a new wife, and they were even having a baby. Mom had wanted to have another baby after me. I had heard her once talking about it with Lisa. She wanted me to be a big sister, but then she was diagnosed with AIDS. Now Dad was having a baby without her. "I wonder if he even cares that she's dead," I said.

"Oh, Emmy," Lisa said. "Of course he does."

I knew Lisa was probably right, but I didn't want to think about Dad anymore. There would be plenty of time for him. I used to see him only every other weekend and for dinner on Tuesday nights. The last couple of months I hadn't seen him as much because Mom didn't feel well and I was spending time with her. Anyway it didn't matter because now I'd be living with him . . . and with Meg, my stepmother, his new wife. I hated thinking about her as my father's wife, since that's what Mom used to be.

I wanted to concentrate on Mom and no one else. I tried to hold a picture of her up in my mind. I was full of Mom, but Mom was gone, so I was full of emptiness. It felt like something sharp was pressing behind my eyes. I squeezed them shut but they still felt raw and open. What happens when you die? Did Mom get to see her mother? I didn't want Mom to be alone, but I didn't want anyone else to get to be with her. I still needed Mom with me. I hooked my arms around my legs like I was hugging them. Lisa moved closer to me so there was hardly any space between us. "It's all right to cry," she said.

I pressed my face hard into my knees. The top of my jeans felt sticky. The inside of my chest hurt like it was bleeding. Was that what it meant to be bleeding internally? I hated blood. I always tried to stay away from sharp things so I wouldn't get cut and start bleeding. Seeing blood always reminded me that I was infected, and most of all I hated this stupid disease. I was curled into a ball and Lisa rocked and rocked me. It was getting cooler. During the day the sun beats down on our front lawn, but the sun had already moved, so it was behind the house and we were sitting in the shade. Soon it would be dark. I didn't want the day to end. At least today I had seen my mother. But tomorrow I wouldn't see her at all, or the day after that, or the day after that, or ever again. I made myself say it in my head: *You will never see Mom again.* I kept my face pressed against my knees for as long as I could, until all the snot and tears made it hard to breathe, and on top of that, I had to pee. I hadn't been to the bathroom since Mom had died. It seemed ridiculous to have to sit up and blow my nose and go to the bathroom. How could I still have to do things like that? I knew later on Lisa would try and make me eat dinner so I could take my pills without getting nauseous, and then I would brush my teeth and change my clothes and get into my bed.

There were so many things to do. I had to keep breathing, and I would have to put things into my mouth and chew and swallow. And I would have to go to the bathroom and go to school. None of it made any sense, since Mom was gone.

And then there were the other things we would have to do because we were still living and Mom was not, like pack everything up and give things away. Right now all of Mom's clothes were still in the big closet in her bedroom. But it would all get packed up. My stuff would be packed up too. The pictures would be taken off the walls. Lisa would go back to New York City, where she lived, and I would go to Dad and Meg's house.

Technically Dad and Meg's house would be my house now too. But *home* was where all Mom's stuff was—the furniture, the pictures. I wasn't sure where I would put all the pictures of Mom. I knew Meg wouldn't want me putting them up on the walls around Dad's house. And what about the rest of Mom's stuff? I wondered how I would squeeze everything important from Mom's house into my one little room at Dad's. We wouldn't have crunchy peanut butter in the fridge anymore. That was something only Mom liked.

From now on, everything I did would be things I did without a mother. No matter how much I wanted her. No matter how much I needed her. Mom was the only one who knew what it was like to have to take pills every day, and to be scared of getting sick, and to feel different. Now I would have to miss Mom too, and I wouldn't even have her to help me. It wasn't fair.

I didn't want to go back in the house without Mom. But I really had to pee. I lifted up my head and wiped my nose with my sleeve, just like a little kid. My mother was the kind of person who always had tissues in her purse. I turned back to Lisa. "I wish you could live here forever," I told her. If Lisa stayed, I could still live in my house. We wouldn't have to clean out Mom's closet or take all of the pictures off the walls. I thought maybe if I said it out loud, it would come true, even though I knew really it was impossible. Lisa lived so far away. She had a husband and a baby. Her husband called every day to check in. I knew he wanted her to go back home.

"Oh, Em, I know," Lisa said. "I'm so sorry."

"How long are you staying?"

"I'll be here until the end of the week," she said.

Did the end of the week mean Friday or Sunday? Friday was only three days away. I really hoped she meant Sunday. Then I thought it was awful of me to be worrying about the difference between Friday and Sunday. My mother had just died, after all.

"Can I stay here with you until you have to leave?" I asked.

"Absolutely," Lisa said.

"I have to go to the bathroom," I told her. I stood up and watched Lisa push herself up from the ground. She wiped her palms on her jeans and put her arm back around my shoulder. We walked up the steps and into the house together. *This is the first time I'm walking into my house without having a mother,* I thought, and then I stepped inside.

Chapter 2

The funeral was two days later. My aunt Laura, my uncle Rob, and my grandfather had all come in the day before, and of course Lisa was still there. The house felt strange, like it was too full. I was still used to it being just Mom and me. I thought maybe if I fell asleep, when I woke up it would turn back to the way it was before. But it was impossible for me to sleep at all.

In the morning the sun came through the window and lit up my room. I had let it get very messy. The clothes I'd worn the past couple of days were on the floor, along with a hundred other things that had been in my closet. It had been hard to figure out what to wear. All those months that Mom was coughing, I didn't think she was dying and I never thought about asking someone to take me to the mall to buy an outfit to wear for the funeral. The thing was, Mom was always the person I went shopping with. I tore everything out of the closet and threw it on the floor. Afterward, I looked at all my clothes lying there. There was no reason to put them away. I was going to have to pack it all up anyway when I moved to Dad's, so I just left them there.

Lisa came in to make sure I was awake, which of course I was. She was holding a cup of coffee. I could see the steam rising off of the top. I watched her step around my clothes carefully so she wouldn't fall and spill the coffee everywhere, but she didn't say anything about the mess. I sat on the edge of my bed with my legs crossed. I was wearing a light gray dress that Mom had bought me a year before, at our favorite store. It had been at the very back of my closet and when I tried it on it was too short, but when I stood in front of the mirror I actually thought it looked better that way. My hair was pulled back tight in a half ponytail. It gave me a little headache but I didn't want to loosen it because I kind of liked the way it felt.

"You're dressed already?" Lisa said. She was still wearing pajamas—leggings and an old shirt of Mom's. It said *Fleetwood Mac: Sold Out* on the back. I nodded. "You look very pretty," she said.

"Thank you," I said.

Lisa sat down next to me on the bed. She put the coffee mug down on my nightstand. Once when I was visiting Dad, I put a can of soda down on one of the side tables and Meg got upset because I didn't use a coaster. She said the wood could get ring stains. But I didn't care if the coffee mug left a mark. Lisa moved her palm across the comforter to smooth it out. I kept thinking, *This is what I will be wearing when my mother is buried.* I was watching Lisa's hand move across the bed, but I was picturing the coffin being lowered into the ground, and me standing next to the grave in my gray dress that was too short, with my hair pulled back too tight. Then I thought of the other outfit—the one Mom was wearing. Lisa had showed me the dress she'd picked out before she had it sent over to the funeral home. It was rose colored and had a tie around the waist. I blinked quickly so I could stop seeing it.

"Do you want to come downstairs?" Lisa asked. "You can have some cereal."

"I'm really not hungry," I told her.

"I know," she said. She stood up and held out her hand. "Come on."

"Is everyone downstairs?"

"Your grandfather went for a walk a little while ago. I think Laura went with him."

"What about Uncle Rob?"

"He was on the phone with someone from his office a few minutes ago," Lisa said.

"His office?"

"Well, it's a weekday," Lisa said.

"Oh yeah," I said. It was hard to remember the difference between weekdays and weekends. I hadn't gone to school in almost a week, and it felt like forever. The last time I was at school, Mom was alive. It was strange that people had to go to school and to work now that she was gone. It still felt like the whole world should have just stopped. But right then, as I was sitting on my bed in the dress I would wear to Mom's funeral, everyone else in the seventh grade was in homeroom.

Lisa was still holding out her hand to me. She shook it a little to remind me it was there, and I took it. We walked out of the room. Lisa's coffee mug was still sitting on my nightstand, but I didn't remind her to take it with her. I don't know why.

I followed Lisa downstairs and into the kitchen. Someone had lined up my pill bottles on the table. That's the thing about AIDS. You can never forget that you have it. Technically I don't even have AIDS—I'm HIV-positive, which means I'm infected but I'm not sick. But I have to take pills every day, like clockwork, to make sure I don't get sick. I take them three times a day—with breakfast, lunch, and dinner. And I have to take them at the exact same times every day, which isn't always the easiest thing to do.

Some people think as long as you take the pills, you'll stay healthy. They think people die of AIDS only if they live in poor countries where they don't have medicine. But it's not that easy. It's just so hard to take medicine all the time. It's like a constant reminder that you're not normal. And some people have really bad side effects, so they can't their pills like they're supposed to. That's what happened with Mom. The medication made her sick, so she couldn't always take the right amount. I only get a little bit sick when I take my pills, and the sick feeling goes away pretty quickly.

At school when I have to take my pills, the nurse doles out the exact dosage, like she doesn't trust me to remember how much to take. But at home it's up to me. I pressed down on the child-safety lock and popped open one of the bottles. When I was little I used to cry every time I had to take my medicine. It tasted so gross and I hated feeling nauseous three times a day. Mom would hold the bottle up and kiss it. "I love this for keeping you well," she would say. I closed my eyes for a second and thought of Mom's voice again. I had learned to swallow pills, so I didn't have to take that awful liquid stuff anymore. But I still hated it.

Uncle Rob was standing in front of the fridge, leaning inside with the door wide open, his cell phone balanced between his ear and his shoulder. "Well that's what you're paid for, buddy," Uncle Rob said. He was speaking loudly, the way he always did. When I was little I asked Aunt Laura what Rob's job was, and she said he put deals together. I pictured him at his office with a deck of cards, dealing them out to a bunch of guys in suits. I still had no idea what his job really was. Uncle Rob turned from the fridge and saw me at the table. "Sorry," he mouthed, and walked out of the room. I heard him start cursing in the hallway.

Lisa put a bowl of cereal in front of me. "Just do your best," she said. I picked up the spoon and pushed down on the flakes floating in the milk. I liked the way they popped back up. Lisa sat down across from me. "Just a few bites, Emmy," she said, like I was a little kid. I felt like a little kid, but I also felt older. I closed my eyes and thought about dipping the spoon back into the bowl, scooping out cereal and bringing it to my mouth, chewing and swallowing. It seemed impossible. My hand felt heavy. I opened my eyes and made myself lift the spoon up in my hand. I dipped it into the bowl and brought the spoon to my mouth. I could still eat. I just didn't want to. "Good girl," Lisa said.

Rob came back into the kitchen. He snapped his cell phone shut and put it in his shirt pocket. He put his hand on my shoulder and tapped his fingers up and down. I took another bite of cereal, but it tasted funny. I could taste the metal from the spoon. I made myself swallow so I wouldn't throw up. "Aunt Laura and I want you to know that you can come to Colorado anytime," Uncle Rob said. "Anytime at all. You can come for Christmas break, if you want. We can go skiing. You'd like that, right?"

"You mean winter break," I said.

"What?"

"You said Christmas break, but they call it winter break, so it includes everyone."

"Christmas, Hanukkah, Kwanzaa, winter break," Uncle Rob said. He pulled out the chair next to me and sat down. "Whatever you want to call it, whenever you want to come, you are welcome." I nodded, even though I didn't want to go to Colorado. Mom had said maybe we would go to Paris. She liked us to have special vacations. She said we needed to take advantage of having time together.

I didn't want the cereal in front of me anymore. "Do you want the rest?" I asked Uncle Rob. He was always hungry. When we would all go out to eat, he would finish his meal and then eat the leftovers off of Aunt Laura's, Mom's, and my plates.

"Sure," he said. I pushed the bowl over to him and he picked up my spoon. The phone rang and Lisa stood up to answer it. I hoped it wasn't Dad. He had called about a dozen times since Mom died, but I didn't want to talk to him. Lisa said he wanted to see me, but I told her to tell him not to come. I figured if he really wanted to see me, he would come over no matter what I said. Besides, I would have to see him at the funeral anyway.

"Em, it's Nicole," Lisa said. Nicole Lister—my best friend. She had also called a bunch of times since Mom died, but I didn't feel like talking. We'd text-messaged each other. She had written, "luv u xox," and I wrote back, "thx luv u 2." Mom used to read over my shoulder when I was texting, and she would laugh because she thought it looked like another language. "MOS!" I would write Nicole, which meant *Mom over shoulder*.

I looked at the clock and thought Nicole should be in French class right then, conjugating verbs or something. Maybe she had snuck into the bathroom and was using her cell phone in a stall, or maybe she told the teacher she was calling me and got special permission to leave class. She seemed like a stranger, in a way. I hadn't seen her since Mom died. I realized that was how I was measuring time—by when Mom died. If the last time I did everything was before Mom died, then she didn't feel as far away. Lisa was still looking at me and I shook my head. "I'm sorry, Nicole," Lisa said. "Emmy can't come to the phone right now." I wondered what Nicole was saying back to her. Lisa hung up. "She says the principal is canceling all the seventh-grade classes this afternoon and she'll see you at the funeral," Lisa said.

"It will be good to see your friends, don't you think?" Uncle Rob said. I nodded even though there was only one person I wanted to see, and she would be in a box.

Uncle Rob finished my cereal and left the room to make another phone call. Lisa put the dishes in the dishwasher. I heard the front door open and close and I knew Grandpa and Aunt Laura were back from their walk. The house was full again. Everyone had to get ready for the funeral, but I was already dressed.

Chapter 3

A little while later a limo came to pick us up. I wondered who had ordered it. I hadn't ever been in one before. It made me think about a movie I'd seen once, where some kids were riding in a limo. They opened up the sunroof and stuck their heads out the top, so they could wave at people in other cars.

It was strange to get to ride in a limo because Mom had died. There we were, all dressed up and in a limo, on our way to a funeral. I ran my fingers across a row of buttons. I pressed the button to roll down the window that divided us from the driver, and then I pressed it again to roll it back up. My grandfather put his hand on mine. I wasn't sure if it was to stop me or just to hold my hand.

Dad was already at the funeral home when we got there. I held Lisa's hand as tightly as I could, and she put her arm around me like she owned me. I knew Lisa hated Dad for leaving Mom and me. Dad stepped forward to hug me. He bent down and wedged his arm between Lisa and me so he could put his arms around me. When he stood back up it looked like he was crying. He hugged my grandfather and Aunt Laura. Uncle Rob shook his hand. "I'm sorry, Bryan," Uncle Rob said to him.

It didn't seem right for Uncle Rob to feel sorry for Dad; after all, Mom wasn't even Dad's wife anymore. "Where's Meg?" I asked, so Uncle Rob would remember that Dad had married someone else.

"She's home," Dad said.

"She's not coming?" Lisa asked. She tightened her grip around me. I wished she would decide to move to Connecticut. Even if her husband and son had to come too, it would be okay. We could all stay in my house.

"She's pregnant," Dad said. "She was afraid to come to the funeral. It's supposed to be bad luck when you're pregnant. And it's her first pregnancy, so she's being extra cautious." He looked down at me. "But she's thinking of you, Emmy. She's been talking about you all week, and she gave me a card to give to you. Do you want it now?"

I shook my head.

The funeral director came out and told us we should go into the family room. People started arriving, and I stood between Lisa and Aunt Laura. We were all lined up so everyone could come in and say hello to us before sitting down in the chapel. Practically the entire seventh grade showed up, along with a lot of the teachers and even Mr. Jennings, the principal. A bunch of the parents came too. Everyone hugged me, even the people who I barely knew. Some people started crying when they saw me. Lisa had put sunglasses on, so when I looked at her I couldn't see her eyes but I could still tell she was crying too.

We went into the chapel last, but the first two rows had been saved for us. It reminded me of going down to the cafeteria at school. Nicole always got to the cafeteria before me because I had to go to the nurse's office to take my pills. That way I could eat right after taking them and I wouldn't get sick. Nicole made sure to save a seat for me next to her. She was always having to do things because I was infected. But when she goes home, she gets to be in a house where no one's infected with anything. I sometimes imagine what it's like to be her.

I knew Nicole was somewhere in the back of the chapel. I wondered if she was sitting with people from school or with her parents. If her parents were there, then who was watching the twins? Nicole has a younger brother and sister, Seth and Riley, who are four years old. They went to preschool in the mornings, but they were home in the afternoons. Maybe the Listers had gotten a babysitter for them, just because of Mom's funeral. That was weird to think about—that Nicole's parents would have to pay someone money so they could be at Mom's funeral. It made me happy in a way. It was proof that Mom was important if the Listers had to give something up to be there for her.

There was organ music playing softly in the background. I sat down next to Lisa, and Dad sat on the other side of me. It didn't make sense that he was in the front row. It was just like when Uncle Rob told Dad he was sorry. I was getting so angry at Dad. I wanted to tell him to go away and sit somewhere else, or to go home and be with his pregnant wife, but I knew everyone was looking at me, so I didn't say anything at all. I just inched closer to Lisa.

The coffin was right in front of me. It was set up on a table with wheels. I sat against Lisa and stared at it. The music faded away and the priest stood and started talking about Mom. "Simone was a mother first," the priest said. "She lived for her daughter. Of course, every mother lives for her children, but Simone faced challenges most of us never have to face. She was infected with a virus—a terrible virus—which she didn't know she had and she unfortunately passed on to her beloved daughter."

I thought about the virus Mom had passed on to me. The human immunodeficiency virus, "HIV" for short. It's not an easy virus to get—you don't just wake up with it one day, like a cold or the flu. You can get it from having sex with someone who's infected, or if your blood gets mixed with blood that already has HIV in it. Or a mom can give it to her baby when she's pregnant or breastfeeding, which is the way I got it. It means I'm HIV-positive, and I could get sick with AIDS. Its real name is acquired immunodeficiency syndrome. People who have it don't have strong immune systems, so their bodies can't fight infections. But that's such a long name, everyone just calls it by its initials: AIDS. It's like a nickname. How could Mom have died of a nickname? It seemed so stupid. She got it from the boyfriend she had right before she met Dad. His name was Travis. He broke up with Mom because he wanted to move to Europe and start a band, and she wanted to get married and have kids. The way she met Dad was he saw her crying about Travis on the street once, and Dad offered to buy her some coffee because she looked so sad and he felt sorry for her. Mom liked him because he was a stable guy with a regular job and not some guy who wanted to be a rock star. She thought he would be a better kind of father than Travis would be. But it was weird, because I ended up inheriting something from Travis, too—the worst, most important thing about me.

I wondered if Travis was still alive, and if he was, I wondered if he felt sorry. Maybe he never even thought about Mom at all. Maybe he took pills and was just fine. It made me hate him.

Mom once told me she didn't hate Travis because she didn't think he knew he was infected with AIDS when he gave it to her.

He didn't look sick at all when Mom was dating him. I didn't look sick at all, but we knew I was infected, so I would probably never get to have sex. Not that it mattered right then, but I knew it would matter later, if I grew up. AIDS would always be in me. It was the thing about me that everyone knew. But it's not like I could actually feel AIDS inside me, so maybe it wasn't real. Maybe my life was just a movie. Maybe it was all pretend, and the funeral director was actually a movie director, and this was the part of the movie where Mom died and I had to act sad at the funeral. But really she wasn't dead at all, and at some point the director would call "Cut!" and I could go home to Mom. Life wasn't as sad when you thought it might be a movie, because then you were just acting instead of really feeling.

The priest was still talking. "Simone never gave up. Even at the end, she was fighting for her health, and for her daughter Emerson—Emmy, as we all know her. She is here today." Dad reached over and squeezed my knee when the priest said that. I felt a chill run up my spine. "Now we can all be grateful to have known this extraordinary woman, this extraordinary mother. And we can be grateful that Simone is at peace now, and that she is with God."

Something was caught in my throat like I was choking. I wasn't grateful for anything at all. What did Father Donaldson know about Mom anyway? We never even went to church. And what did he know about God? It's not like he could see God. He couldn't know for sure they were together. He couldn't even know for sure that God existed.

The whole being-with-God thing didn't make me grateful at all. Even if he was real, I still wanted Mom to be with me.

Lisa had told me I could speak about Mom if I wanted, but I said I didn't. Other people stood up to give speeches. Someone from the hospital spoke, and Aunt Laura read a poem. Afterward, the music started up again. It wasn't the organ music this time. It was a song by one of Mom's favorite singers, Sheryl Crow. We used to listen to her CDs in the car. My favorite songs were the ones that sounded like rock and roll. When Nicole was there, she and I would bring our fists to our mouths, like we were holding microphones, and really belt it out. But Mom liked the slower songs. I wondered if she had picked out the music to play at the funeral and told Lisa, or maybe even Father Donaldson. The song that was playing had a line about the sun shining and burning away the darkness. I listened to Sheryl Crow singing. I knew her voice so well because we played her CD a thousand times. And then I realized something—the next time Sheryl Crow had a new CD out, Mom wouldn't know. She would never get to hear it.

Uncle Rob and one of Mom's doctors stepped forward and began pulling the table with Mom's coffin down the center aisle.

"Come on, Emmy," Dad said.

"What?" I asked. "What?" I felt like I didn't understand. It was like normal words didn't make sense anymore. I wasn't sure what to do.

"Emmy," Lisa said softly. "It's time to go, sweetheart." I looked up at her. She wasn't wearing her sunglasses anymore. There were faint gray lines on her face where the mascara had run. I stood up to be next to her, and she pulled me down the aisle, so we were following Mom as she was wheeled through the crowd and outside. The coffin was loaded into one of those special cars for funerals. Mom's name was spelled out in white letters on a little black plaque in the window.

Someone slammed the door shut. I couldn't see in through the windows and I missed being close to the coffin. I hadn't realized that I wanted to be near it until it was loaded into the car.

Aunt Laura put her arm around my shoulders. We got back into the limo and drove over to the cemetery. The limo pulled up to the edge of the grass, where all the people were buried. We walked along a little path, and I looked at the names on the headstones. There was a hole already dug for Mom. I knew someone had probably ordered the stone that would say SIMONE DAVIS PRICE, 1963–2008. Then I imagined the way my name would look on one of the headstones: EMERSON LOUISE PRICE. I was born in 1995, and I wondered what the second date would be. I hoped I could be buried next to Mom. I wouldn't mind being there now. I wanted to be as close to her as possible. I thought about how I could jump into the hole for Mom right then. But then someone would jump in after me to rescue me. I didn't want to be rescued.

Dad was watching me. I was glad he didn't know what I was thinking. It made it seem like he didn't know anything about me. "It's gonna be okay, Emmy. We're gonna make it through this," he said. "I'm gonna be here for you. I promise."

But my mother's coffin was about to be lowered into the ground, and Dad had left me once before. I wasn't sure I could believe him.

Chapter 4

It almost seemed like it should stay April forever, just because Mom wasn't there to see May. But time kept passing. It was the first new month without Mom, and I finally had to go back to school.

Highlands Middle School looked bigger and cleaner than the last time I'd been there, which made no sense because it was the same old school, with the same old linoleum floors. My shoes made the same slapping noise as I walked down the hall to my locker. I thought maybe I wouldn't remember the combination for my locker, but when I got there I turned the dials and it popped open just like before.

I was usually a pretty good student. Mom always made sure I did my homework and studied before tests. But I'd missed so much work and I felt completely lost in all my classes. I wasn't used to feeling that way. It made me feel dizzy.

I had to go to the nurse's office during lunch to take my pills. She keeps bottles of my pills in her medicine cabinet, so I can take them every day. She also keeps a box of latex gloves in her office—just like the kind doctors use—in case I get cut and need help with a Band-Aid. That way she won't have to touch my blood. She says she uses the gloves for everyone, but I know they're really there for me.

There were a couple of other kids waiting in the nurse's office when I got there, but since I have to take my medicine at the same time every day, she let me skip ahead of them. "Welcome back, Emmy," Ms. Taylor said.

"Thanks," I said. She brought me a little cup of water so I could swallow the pills. I knew everyone was watching me. I swallowed quickly, and it felt like one of the pills was caught in my throat.

I went down to the cafeteria and sat next to Nicole. She was talking to Rachel, Isabella, and Julia. They're girls in our grade who we hang out with sometimes. Rachel was saying something about our French teacher, Mrs. Burkle. In class, we're supposed to call her *Madame* Burkle, but Rachel hates doing that because French is her least favorite subject. It's like she's getting back at her by calling her "Mrs." instead of "Madame." "Did you see the hat she had on today?" Rachel asked. Mrs. Burkle wore a hat every day, even though there was a rule against students wearing hats inside, which is what Dad would call a double standard. "It was this weird flower print. It kind of looked like she had a curtain on top of her head."

"Do you think that she's really bald and she doesn't want to wear a wig?" Isabella asked.

"But she has a ponytail," Julia said.

"She could be bald just on top," Isabella said.

"Yeah, like Mr. Jennings," Rachel said. They all laughed. I knew I could join the conversation if I wanted to, but I didn't have anything to say. It was weird, because I was glad they were around me. There was no way I wanted to sit alone at lunch. But I didn't know how to act the way I used to. A few minutes later, the bell rang, signaling that the period was over.

I felt just as lost in my afternoon classes as I had that morning. My English class was finishing up a discussion on a book I'd never heard of, and it was impossible to pay attention. I sat at my desk and tried to look like I was listening and thinking about the book. I scrunched up my eyebrows and looked toward Mrs. Carrion, and every time she called on someone, I turned my head to look at whoever was talking. But I don't think I heard a word anyone said.

Mrs. Carrion had given me a copy of the book I'd never heard of, and I turned it over in my hands. I wondered if Mom had ever read it. She loved to read. I thought of the stack of books she kept on her nightstand. I wondered what the last book she ever read was. Did she get to finish it? What if she didn't finish it? What if she died without knowing the ending? What was the last sentence she ever read?

When the bell rang, I pulled my bag off the floor and onto my lap. I put the book in my bag to bring home. I'm a fast reader and English is my best subject. I knew I could probably catch up, but I wasn't sure if I would even bother. I stood up and followed the crowd toward the door. "Emmy, can you stay a minute?" Mrs. Carrion asked. I felt my chest tighten, but I stepped back from the door. I hoped I wasn't about to get into trouble because I hadn't been paying attention. Dad and Meg wouldn't understand at all.

Mrs. Carrion waited until everyone else had left the room. She leaned up against her desk and took off her glasses. They dangled from a red chain on her neck. Mom's favorite color was red. That's why she had a red car. Ever since she died I hadn't been able to look at anything or anyone without thinking it had something to do with Mom. It was like everything was a sign of her. I didn't mind because I liked feeling like she was around.

"I just wanted to say I am so sorry, Emmy," Mrs. Carrion said. "I wanted to be there for you at the funeral, but my son was sick that day."

"That's okay," I said.

"Did you get the basket the English department sent?" Mrs. Carrion asked.

"What?"

"We sent a basket of food," she said.

We'd gotten about a dozen baskets of food. Meg had taken all the cards and put them on Dad's desk so he would know where to send the acknowledgment cards. I hadn't read any of them. "Oh yeah," I said. "Thanks. It was great."

"Good," Mrs. Carrion said. She fingered the red chain around her neck. "You know, Emmy, I lost my mother when I was young, too. I was a little bit older than you are now, but I know what you're going through."

I knew she couldn't really know what I was going through. Her mother probably had cancer, or some disease like that, which meant Mrs. Carrion didn't have to take pills herself every day. And I bet she didn't have to move out of her house when her mother died. My bag was getting heavy. I shifted it to my other shoulder, but that felt worse. I usually carry my bag on my right shoulder. "I have history now," I said.

"I don't mean to keep you," Mrs. Carrion said. "But come see me anytime. My door is always open." I wondered what door she meant. The door to the faculty lounge was closed to students at all times.

"Thanks," I said again.

I walked down the hall to history. Class had just started, and when I walked in everyone turned in their seats to look at me. We don't have assigned seats in history, but I always sat in the same seat—in the second row, between Nicole and Rachel. Except this time Rachel was sitting in the seat next to Nicole, and someone else was sitting in the seat that is usually Rachel's. I guess that's what happens when your mother dies and you miss three weeks of school.

I looked down at the floor and walked to a desk in the back of the room. I pulled my notebook out of my bag and pretended to pay attention again. Every so often someone would turn around to look at me. Whenever they caught my eye, they'd smile and quickly turn back around. Finally the bell rang. I was so glad it was three o'clock, even though I didn't really want to go home to Meg. I wished she had a job in an office, like Dad did, so she wouldn't be home. I'd been to Dad's office a few times—it's in one of those buildings where the glass looks likes mirrors from the outside. I used to love how shiny it was. But Meg did something with graphic design and spent the day in front of a computer in her study. She hardly ever had to leave the house.

It's not that I hated Meg. She was usually nice to me. But being around her so much made me feel like I was cheating on Mom, or something like that. Also, I was mad at Meg for not coming to Mom's funeral.

Nicole came up to me after class. "I wasn't sure you were coming," she said. "I would've saved your seat."

"You knew I was in school. We had lunch."

"Yeah, but you were so quiet and you hardly ate at all, and then you were late to class," she said. "I thought maybe you felt bad and went home."

"I'm fine," I told her.

"Good," she said. "Can I still come over?"

"If you want to," I said. It occurred to me that I could never be really sure if I had any friends—not even Nicole. People had to be nice to me because I was the one with the saddest life. If my family was healthy, life would be completely different.

"Obviously I want to," she said. "I just have to stop by my locker to get something. I'll meet you in the front in two secs."

I walked to the front and leaned against the building. Nicole always took longer than she said she would. I knew people were looking at me and I wished Nicole would hurry up. She came up from behind me and put her arm around my shoulder. "All right, let's go," she said.

We walked the whole way to Dad's house. I knew Meg was home because her car was in the driveway, but she was probably working in her study, so I opened the door with my key. Dad had given me a key a couple of years before, but I didn't use it until Mom died. I used to go into his house only if he was with me.

Nicole and I went up to my room, which I've always called "my room at Dad's house." Even though I had moved in, I still thought of it as "my room at Dad's house," and the room that was just "my room," my real room, was my room at Mom's house. But my real room was in a house that now had a FOR SALE sign on the front lawn. It didn't even look like my room anymore. Some of the furniture was still there, but all the stuff that had been in my drawers and on the bookshelves was now in my room at Dad's house. I'd also taken all of the photos Mom had kept on her dresser. I took them out of their frames and put them all in an envelope. It was in a drawer next to my bed.

Nicole flopped onto my bed. She has the kind of hair that flops whenever she flops. It's really long and thick. My hair comes down to just below my shoulders, so it doesn't flop as much. I guess it's thicker than average, but not nearly as thick as Nicole's. "So?" she said.

"So," I said.

"I like your new room," she said. I shrugged. My *new* room.

It wasn't really new. Dad and Meg had moved into the house a couple of years before, and it had been my room at Dad's house the whole time. I'd picked out most of the things in it—Dad had taken me shopping and let me choose the furniture and the bedding and the light blue paint for the walls. Now I had some stuff from Mom's house in it too. But it still seemed like it wasn't my room. Actually I hated it. I wanted my real room back.

I didn't know how to explain that to Nicole, but it felt weird to talk about my room like it was just a regular thing. It felt like we were talking around Mom. I was living in my room at Dad's house because Mom was dead, but we weren't really talking about how Mom was dead. I could tell Nicole felt weird too. There was a quiet between us that wasn't usually there. I took a deep breath.

"Well, I brought you something," Nicole said finally.

"Is it a basket of food?" I asked. Nicole looked at me funny. "I'm just kidding," I said.

"It's way better than food," she said. She bent down over her bag. "Now close your eyes," she said. I closed my eyes. My lids felt heavy, like I could fall asleep right then, just sitting up on my bed while Nicole was rustling through her backpack. "Okay," she said. "Open them."

I opened my eyes. Nicole was holding out a black-and-white photo. She was grinning so hard it looked like the edges of her mouth must hurt.

"It's Brody Hudson," Nicole said. Her voice was almost a squeal. "And it's autographed. See, look at his handwriting. Just think: Brody Hudson actually held this exact picture in his hands and now I'm holding it in my hands. Maybe he even held it when he was on the set of a new movie he's filming or something. Can you just imagine? Maybe other famous people held it too!"

"Maybe," I said.

"Anyway," Nicole said. "I just really wanted to give you something to cheer you up. I know it's dumb, but I joined Brody Hudson's fan club a couple of months ago, and they sent me this picture."

I knew the picture had to be one of her favorite things, and it was really nice of her to give it to me, even if I wasn't quite as obsessed with Brody Hudson as she was. Actually, I tried not to think about boys as much as Nicole did, even though there was a boy at school that I sort of liked. His name was Aaron Bay. But I knew he would probably never like me, not the way boys are supposed to like girls.

Nicole was looking at me expectantly. I knew she really wanted me to like the picture. "It's great," I said. "Thanks." I smiled so she would think that I meant it.

"You're welcome," she said. "I figured since you had a new room, you'd need to decorate it. It'll look good on the wall."

"Tell me where I should put it."

Nicole jumped up and held the picture up against each wall. "He looks good wherever you put him," she reported. She puckered up her lips and brought Brody Hudson's face up to her mouth. "Oh, I wish this were really my first kiss. I wish my first kiss could be with Brody."

"If he ever met you, I'm sure he'd want to kiss you."

"Stop it," she said, but I could tell she liked that I'd said that. "What do you think Brody is doing right now?" she asked.

"I have no idea."

"I think he's walking around somewhere very cool in Hollywood, and people are following him and taking his picture. But he's just acting cool, like he doesn't even notice."

I wondered if being famous was like being in school after your mother dies, with everyone staring at you. I could understand why some famous people hate all the attention, and you see pictures of them with their hands up to block the photographer. Sometimes you just don't want to be looked at. But at least famous people got to decide that they wanted to be famous in the first place, and they could wear amazing clothes and have everyone love them and think they're beautiful. They could live anywhere they wanted too.

There was a knock on the door and then it just opened, even though we didn't say *Come in.* "Hello," Meg called.

"Hi," Nicole said.

"How was school?" she asked.

"Fine," I said.

"Well, I'm sorry to interrupt," Meg said. "I wanted to let you know there are some fresh-baked cookies for you downstairs—my own recipe. I halved the sugar, and you can't even tell the difference. I just pulled them out of the oven, so they're still warm."

Meg was a health nut and nothing she made ever tasted the way it was supposed to, no matter what she said. "You didn't have to do that," I said.

"I wanted to," Meg said. "I'm nesting."

"What?"

"It's what happens when you're pregnant. You start wanting to make a 'nest' for the baby, so you clean the house and hang curtains and bake things," Meg said. Suddenly I wondered if Meg had cleaned the house and baked things when the rest of us were at Mom's funeral. "I'll help you get organized in your room if you want," she said.

"That's okay," I said.

"Well, you seem to have done a good job on your own anyway. I can't believe how many books you have." I'd taken all the books that were in my room at Mom's house, and some of the ones Mom had on her bookshelves. Also Mom had bought a bunch of books she wanted me to read—books she wanted me to read now, and books for adults that she wanted me to have later on. She gave them to Lisa to give to me. I wondered when Mom had picked them out. She must have known she was going to die soon, so she went to the bookstore to get me the books. I imagined her bringing the stack of books to the counter to pay. The cashier wouldn't have known the reason Mom was buying them. She would've just taken Mom's money and put the books in a bag.

"Ooh, the baby's moving," Meg said. "Do you want to feel, Emmy Lou?" It was the name Dad sometimes called me. I didn't like when Meg used it.

"No thanks," I said.

"Can I feel?" Nicole asked. "I love babies."

"Sure," Meg said. She wedged herself onto the bed between Nicole and me. The mattress sunk down when Meg sat. Meg pulled up her shirt around her belly. There was an ugly dark line down the center of Meg's stomach. I thought it was gross that Nicole wanted to touch it.

"What do you mean, you love babies?" I asked. "You're not that into Seth and Riley."

"They're not babies anymore," Nicole said. She let Meg take her hand and place it on her stomach, so she was touching that weird dark line. "Come on, Baby," Nicole said. "Kick me."

"There it is," Meg said. "Can you feel it?"

"Yeah, I totally can," Nicole said. "It's so cool. It's a girl, right?"

"It's a girl," Meg said. They were sitting so close to each other. I felt like I was watching them from outside, like I wasn't even part of the scene. I wondered if somehow Mom could see us. If she saw me sitting next to Meg, would she be upset? I'd never actually heard Mom say that she hated Meg. Once, when I told Mom about how Meg had flipped out when I didn't use a coaster, Mom rolled her eyes and said, "What a perfectionist. Just wait until she has children." And then she got really quiet and walked away, so I knew thinking of Meg having children with Dad had made her sad. And now there I was, sitting next to Meg, who was so obviously pregnant. If Mom was looking down at us, I knew she'd be upset. She might even think she'd been replaced. Just in case, I thought I shouldn't be too nice to Meg. I wanted Mom to know I was still hers. I would never trade her for Meg.

Nicole took her hand off Meg's stomach. "What's her name going to be?" she asked.

"Well, I have a favorite name, and Bryan has a different favorite name, so Emmy will be the deciding vote."

"Did you decide yet?" Nicole asked.

I shook my head. I hadn't, and now I didn't really care about naming a baby that wouldn't even be related to Mom. It wasn't fair that Dad and Meg got to have a baby and Mom didn't. Maybe I wouldn't even love it.

"You have only three and a half months left to choose," Meg said to me. That was the other thing about the baby—it was going to be born right around Mom's birthday. It was supposed to come a couple weeks before, and it didn't seem right.

"What are the choices?" Nicole asked.

"That's a secret," Meg said. "Only Emmy, Bryan, and I know. Right, Em?"

I shrugged. I thought it was dumb that she was making us keep the names a secret. I wanted to tell Nicole, but if I did I knew she'd go on and on about which one was her favorite, and I really didn't want to talk any more about the baby. "What's that line on your stomach, Meg?" I asked.

"It's from the pregnancy," Meg said. "A lot of women get it."

"Does it go away?" Nicole asked.

"Oh, yeah," Meg said. "At least I hope so."

I picked up a pen from the table beside my bed and drew a line across my palm.

"Don't do that, honey," Meg said. "I always get nervous the ink will seep into your blood."

"Does that really happen?" Nicole asked.

"I doubt it," I said.

Meg grunted and pushed herself up from the bed the way pregnant women do. "Well, I'll let you two alone. But come downstairs and have some cookies while they're still warm."

"Thanks," Nicole said.

I watched Meg walk out the door and then I stood up and closed it.

"That's nice that she made us cookies," Nicole said.

I picked up my pen again and drew the line on my hand even darker. "If you can call them that," I said. "You heard her—she cuts the sugar out of the recipe."

"Yeah, I guess," Nicole said. Suddenly she grinned. "Hey, do you think if I made cookies for Brody Hudson and sent them to him that he'd write me a thank-you note? Not just a signed picture, but an actual note thanking me?" she asked.

"Not if they were Meg's cookies," I said.

"No, I mean cookies with the right amount of sugar, or even extra sugar. Really delicious cookies."

"He'd probably worry that they were poisoned and throw them away anyway," I told her.

"Oh, I just know if he ever actually met me, he'd really, really like me. Quick, give me your cell phone. I left mine at home and I promised Rachel I'd text her and let her know when I gave you the picture."

"You're crazy," I said. I was tired of talking about Brody Hudson. I opened my backpack and gave Nicole the phone, and then I picked up the picture of Brody and held it out. I thought about kissing it like Nicole had. It was easier for her. She wasn't infected with anything. When it was time for her first kiss, no one would be afraid for Nicole to kiss them back. It's not like you can even get AIDS from kissing someone, but I knew boys would still be scared of me.

Nicole slid behind me. She put down the phone and wrapped her arms around me. "If you're my best friend, then you must be crazy too," she said.

"I guess I am," I told her.

Chapter 5

It got really warm the next week, and Nicole thought we should picnic outside instead of eating in the cafeteria. "I have to go to the nurse and take my pills," I reminded her.

"So go to the nurse," Nicole said. "I'll go get us some turkey sandwiches, unless the turkey's too slimy-looking. What's your second choice?"

I shrugged. "I don't care," I said.

"All right, I'll get you whatever doesn't look too gross, and meet you on the front lawn, okay?"

"Okay," I said. "Thanks."

Nicole had her hair twisted up on top of her head and fastened with a clip. She undid the clip and shook her head so her hair tumbled down around her face. It was so thick that you couldn't see the part. She swept it back with her hand. "Do you think my hair looks better this way?"

"It looks good," I said. "It always looks good."

Nicole grinned. "I'll meet you in front in five."

I walked down the hall to Ms. Taylor's office. There was a kid lying on the cot at the back of her room. He still had his sneakers on but the laces were undone. I wondered if they were always like that or if he loosened them to be more comfortable. "Hello Emmy," Ms. Taylor said. She didn't whisper, even though the kid in the back seemed to be trying to sleep. "I was just on the phone with your father."

"Why?" I asked, lowering my voice even though she wasn't. I hoped she hadn't been talking so loudly when she was on the phone with Dad. Wasn't there a law about protecting kids' privacy?

"He called about refills for your prescriptions. You know, we're going to be done with these next week." She held up one of the bottles and shook it. I heard the pills inside banging against each other, like maracas. It was funny that she said *we're going to be done*, even though I was the only one who had to swallow them.

"Oh," I said.

Ms. Taylor popped open the pill bottles and lined up my pills. "Let me get you some water and we'll get you out of here. It's beautiful today, isn't it?"

"Yeah," I said. I picked up the first pill and placed it on my tongue.

I had to take three pills in all, which doesn't sound like much, but they were really big pills—the kind that tend to get stuck in your throat. I used the whole glass of water that Ms. Taylor had given me. Afterward I went to the front lawn to meet Nicole. She wasn't there when I got there, and I walked over to the big maple tree in the center of the lawn. On one side of the tree all the roots are really thick, but on the other side the ground is pretty smooth. I always wondered why the sides didn't match up. I sat on the grass on the smooth side of the tree, which was the side in the shade. I was looking at the ground so I heard Nicole's voice before I saw her. "Get up, Em. Come out into the sun. I brought a beach towel."

"Seriously?"

"Yup. I knew it was going to be warm out."

"You think of everything."

Nicole whipped the towel out of her bag and spread it out. She kicked off her shoes and plopped down, and I sat down next to her. "The turkey was incredibly gross-looking today," she said. "You don't even want to know how gross it was. Maybe they spray it overnight so it doesn't go bad or something. It was so slimy. It was like there was this layer of green slime on top of the actual turkey."

I put my hands over my ears and squeezed my eyes shut. Sometimes when people describe something that's really disgusting, I have to close my eyes to get the image of it out of my head.

"Don't worry," Nicole said, pulling at my hand so I could hear her. "I got you a bagel with butter and an apple instead."

"Much better," I said. "Thanks."

"Now we can get tan," Nicole said. She positioned herself so her face was toward the sun. "I'd like a perfect tan by the time school lets out."

"You've got about a month then," I said.

"I know," Nicole said. "I'm counting."

The butter on my bagel was too thick on one side, and Nicole hadn't brought me a knife to spread it out. I rubbed the halves of the bagel together to try and smooth the butter out, and then I took a bite. It seemed extra chewy. "How come food at school never tastes like it's supposed to?" I asked.

"It's amazing that they can even screw up a bagel, but eat the apple," Nicole said. "They couldn't have messed that up."

What was that expression? *An apple a day keeps the doctor away.* That certainly wouldn't apply to me. I ate it anyway since I had to eat something.

"So did I tell you about Seth's latest obsession?" Nicole asked. I shook my head and swallowed a bite of apple. "Well, he thinks if he blows on flowers, he can make them grow faster."

"What?"

"Honestly," Nicole said, "he's nuts. He was watching one of those kids' channels the other day and there was something about planting things and making them grow. And the guy said you have to give plants a lot of love and fresh air. So Seth thought that meant he had to blow on them."

"That's so cute," I said.

"It was at first, but now he's got Riley doing it too. The two of them walk around the house blowing on everything that's green. When they walk down the street, they bend down to blow on the flowers. I had to walk them to school this morning, and it took, like, twice as long because they were stopping to blow on everything."

"At least it's better than when he used to say 'poop' all the time," I said.

"Oh, he still does that," Nicole said. "This morning my mom asked him if he wanted pancakes, and he said he wanted 'poopcakes,' and then he laughed hysterically. You know how he gets when he just cracks himself up. He's so bizarre. I wonder if all boys were that weird when they were little."

"Probably," I said.

"Yeah," Nicole said. "Anyway, do you know who was in front of me in line?"

"Where?" I asked.

"In the cafeteria," she said. "Do you know who was in front of me?"

"Who?"

"Zach Andrews," she said.

"That guy from math?" I asked.

"Yup," she said. "What do you think of him?"

"I don't think I've ever thought anything about him," I said.

"Well, I think he's totally cute," Nicole said. "I think he's totally brodable, actually."

"What do you mean?"

"Oh, 'brodable' is my new word when a boy is as cute as Brody Hudson. Not that anyone could really be *that* cute. But, you know, I think Zach Andrews is close to it at least. Do you think Zach is brodable?"

"I guess," I said.

"Well, he's the most brodable boy in our grade, don't you think?"

"I don't know," I said. I hated talking about Brody Hudson and Zach Andrews. I hated talking about any boy as a matter of fact. Talking about Seth was fine, but that was different because he was Nicole's brother, and besides, he was only four. I didn't like talking about boys my own age. I had never even told Nicole about Aaron Bay. As far as I was concerned, Aaron was even cuter than Zach. But I didn't want to tell Nicole that.

If I didn't have AIDS, I would've told her, and she and I would probably be fighting over who was more brodable. I could just hear her saying, "No way, Em. Zach is *so* much more brodable." She would flip her hair and laugh at me, and I would tell her she was being crazy. It was strange to think about— like getting a glimpse of what my life would be like, if only I were like everyone else. I was just sitting there in the sun with Nicole, and for a moment life didn't feel so sad. But that's the problem with having AIDS. You can maybe get a little glimpse of what it's like to be normal, but then the truth about your life comes crashing back. And that meant I couldn't sit in the sun and have a simple conversation with my best friend about having a crush on a boy. I couldn't talk about it without thinking all sorts of sad and scary things. I probably wouldn't ever have a boyfriend. If I grew up, nobody would want to be my husband. You have to have sex with your wife, and who would want to be married to someone who could pass on a terrible disease, someone who might die and leave them all alone? Then again, maybe I wouldn't get to grow up after all.

"So I guess you don't think Zach's that cute," Nicole said.

"I think he's cute," I said.

"No you don't," Nicole said, and she sounded sort of upset about it. "I can tell by your face that you don't."

"We don't have to agree on everything," I said.

"So you think I'm crazy for liking him."

"I didn't say that," I said.

"No, really," Nicole said.

"Well, maybe just boy crazy," I said. "Lately it's all you want to talk about."

"My mom says that's normal," Nicole said.

In my head I repeated the two most important words: "mom," "normal."

Nicole reached up and pulled on my arm, so I had to lie down next to her. I turned my face to the sun, like she did. When I closed my eyes, it was still bright, as though I were looking straight at the sun. "Do you remember that movie my mom rented for us when we were little?" Nicole asked. "The one with the mouse that got lost and couldn't find his family? What was it called—*An American Tail?* We must have watched it a hundred times."

I opened my eyes again. "Yeah, I remember," I said. "Why? Do you want to rent it for Seth and Riley?"

"Maybe, but do you remember the song?"

"I don't know," I said.

"Oh come on," Nicole said. "We used to sing it all the time, remember? We took my mom's hairbrushes and pretended they were microphones, and we each sang the different parts." She smiled like she was thinking about it, remembering everything.

"I remember," I said. We had made up a dance to go with the song and put on a show for our parents. "We always wanted to be rock stars, and we thought we sounded so good. Like we could be famous."

Nicole let out a laugh that didn't sound like her regular laugh. Maybe it sounded different because she was lying down. "Yeah," she said. "We even had stage names for ourselves, in case we were discovered. I remember mine was Victoria Magenta. What was yours again?"

"Crystal Rose Featherwoman," I said. At first I had wanted my last name to be Featherman, but Nicole had said since I was a woman, it should be Feather*woman*.

"God, we were lame," she said. "But I was just thinking about it. You know, looking up at the sky. Remember that line in the song? The one about how we're all looking at the same big sky?"

I looked up at the sky. It was totally blue. I think sky blue is my favorite color, but it's hard to know exactly what color that is, since the sky is always changing.

"It's amazing, isn't it?" Nicole said. "The same big sky. We're all connected, you know? What do you think Brody Hudson is doing right now?"

"I don't know," I said. I was thinking about Mom in the sky and being all connected. *I love you to the sky.* I wondered what Mom was doing right then. Mother's Day had been over the weekend, but I didn't celebrate it because I didn't have a mother. The wind blew suddenly, gently. I wondered if it was her. It felt like it meant something, like it was magic.

"You're so quiet today," Nicole said.

"Sorry," I said.

"It's okay," she said. She turned to look at me and propped her head up on her hand. "It's just strange. Don't you want to talk to me?"

"I just don't feel like sitting around here talking about stupid boys," I said.

"That's not all we're talking about," Nicole said.

"It feels like it is," I said.

"Fine," Nicole said. She moved so she was sitting up completely and looking down at me. "We don't have to talk about boys. We can talk about whatever you want."

"I don't really feel like talking about anything," I told her.

"Oh, you're thinking about your mom, aren't you?" Nicole said softly.

I shrugged. Nicole looked so sweet and worried. I didn't want to be mean to her. All of a sudden I felt like I was going to cry. It was really the last thing I wanted to do. We were right in front of school and other people might see me. I knew Nicole would be really nice if I started crying, because she always was. She would give me a hug and tell me everything would be okay. I knew I should feel lucky to have a friend like Nicole, but it was just so hard to feel lucky about anything. No matter how nice Nicole was, she wouldn't really understand. How could she? She was healthy and she had a mother who she got to see all the time, even on Mother's Day, and she still got to live in her house.

But the only life I knew was one where things could disappear.

It was so unfair. Why me? Why us? I turned away from Nicole and I could see other kids off in the distance, hanging out, laughing, doing homework. There were so many other families out there. It could've happened to someone else instead. It's not like I wanted anything bad to happen to anyone else, but I wanted things to be okay for Mom and me even more.

"I'm sorry," Nicole said. "I didn't know, really. And I don't want to remind you about your mom if you're not thinking about it."

"I'm always thinking about it," I said. It wasn't exactly true. There were a few moments when I hadn't been thinking about it, like when we were talking about Seth and Riley. But even when I wasn't actually thinking about it, it was always so close. Mom was just there, at the edge of my mind, like she was waiting right behind my eyes. It felt like my job to be remembering all the time.

"I'm sorry," Nicole said again. "It's just that when Dakota died, it was harder for me when I talked about it too much. It was better when people didn't remind me how much I missed her."

"Dakota was just a dog," I said. "She was just a stupid dog."

Nicole moved back a little from me, like I'd hit her. I'd never said anything like that to her before. The words echoed in my head. It didn't even sound like my voice. We stared at each other for a couple seconds. I could tell she didn't know what to say to me. Finally she took a deep breath. "My mom said you might be really mad for a while," she said. "I totally get that. I know you must miss your mom a lot. But it's not my fault that she died."

I felt that feeling you get right before you start to cry, when something is pressing behind your eyes and suddenly they seem really big and wide open. I didn't say anything. I just stood up and turned to walk away.

"Em," Nicole said. "Emmy, please don't go."

I could tell she had started to cry, but I didn't turn back around. It wasn't fair that she was crying. After all, everything was still the same for her. I knew that none of it was Nicole's fault and I shouldn't be mean to her. But I hated everyone who didn't have to worry about AIDS, and I just kept walking.

Chapter 6

I walked across the lawn and through the gate at the front entrance. There are a couple of benches just outside the gate. Sometimes there are teachers sitting on them during lunch—I think they hang out there to try and catch kids who are sneaking off school grounds. But that day nobody was there, and I made a left onto the sidewalk and kept going.

I felt light. It was strange, like I was getting away with something. For a second I felt like I could do anything and it wouldn't matter. The thing is, I hadn't actually meant to just walk out of school like that. It's not like I even knew where I was going. But before I knew it, I was heading home—to my old home, my real home. The last time I walked home from school to Mom's house was the week before she died. It was the middle of April and it was still cold enough to need a jacket. Now I was in just a T-shirt and the trees looked so green and fresh.

I had made the walk to Mom's house about a thousand times. It seemed so natural to be walking there, so normal. I almost didn't have to concentrate on where I was going. I made another left and started skipping for no reason at all. I probably hadn't skipped anywhere since the first grade, but I skipped the whole way back to Mom's house.

I stopped as soon as I got to the house. My heart was thumping in my chest. I knew it was only partly because I was out of breath from skipping. The FOR SALE sign was still posted at the front. I hated that sign, like the house could be for anyone. But no one was supposed to live in the house besides Mom and me. I started to walk up the front walkway. It was made out of the same cement as the sidewalk, and I counted each of the squares. I hadn't ever done that before, so I didn't know exactly how many squares there were between the sidewalk and the front stoop. It seemed like the kind of thing I should know about my own house. I felt like I should be memorizing everything. There were seven squares between the sidewalk and the front stoop. Lucky number seven. I wondered if that meant anything. Another sign from Mom, like I was supposed to be there.

The front door was locked, of course. I wished I had my key. But all I had was the key to Dad's house. I pulled it out of my bag and tried to fit it in the lock anyway, but it didn't work. How is it possible that every single door in the world has a different key? I fingered Dad's key in my hand. There couldn't really be that many different shapes to be able to make a totally unique key for every single lock. Maybe there was another house out there that would open with the exact same key as Dad's house.

But Dad's key was useless at Mom's house. I shoved it into my pocket and put my hand around the doorknob. I knew it wouldn't budge if I tried to turn it, but I tried anyway. I twisted and pulled, but nothing happened. Wasn't there a way to open doors with a credit card? I'd seen it on television. You slip the credit card in the little crack between the door and the frame, and somehow it tricks the lock into opening. It didn't matter anyway, since I didn't have one.

I walked around to the side of the house. Dad was still paying the gardener to come every couple of weeks, because that's what you do when you're trying to sell a house—you make sure everything stays clean and pretty. The grass was neatly cut and there were multicolored pansies by the walkway. Mom and I had planted flowers in the exact same place the summer before.

I went back out to the front of the house and sat on the stoop. Maybe the real estate agent would come by to show the house to someone, and I'd get to go inside. I wasn't sure if I wanted her to or not. It would've been so good to be back inside my house, but then I would've had to be there with strangers. Strangers who didn't understand that the house would always belong to Mom and me. Our furniture was still inside the house because that was another thing you did when you were trying to sell a house—you made it look like people still lived there. At least that's what Dad told me. He said people were more likely to buy a house when they could see the furniture and imagine living there themselves.

Just thinking about it made me feel sick. I hated Dad for leaving our stuff in the house for other people to look at. And I hated the real estate agent and everyone she brought in to see the house. All those people who were looking to buy a new house. They would come in and look at our furniture, go through the rooms and imagine living in them, and think about things they would do to change them. They wouldn't think about Mom at all. It wasn't right.

But nobody came to look at the house while I was sitting there on the stoop. I didn't even see any of our neighbors. I guess it was a good thing, since someone might have told Dad that I was there. Being there alone sort of felt like being in a parallel universe. It all looked the same, but everything was different.

I still thought I should be able to move back into the house on my own. It wasn't sold yet, so it wasn't like anyone else was expecting to live there. We could take the FOR SALE sign off the front lawn. Dad was paying for the gardeners, and I could take care of the inside of the house on my own. I could use our furniture since it was all still there. I could cook for myself. I could keep things clean. I knew it was stupid and there were laws against thirteen-year-olds living alone, but it wasn't fair. It should depend on the thirteen-year-old. Maybe some kids weren't ready to live by themselves, but I was. *It's my house,* I thought. *Mine. I should get to live in my own house.* I knew it would be better than living somewhere I didn't want to be. Besides, I felt more alone at Dad's house, even with him and Meg there.

I tried to think of my life like a movie again. If it were a movie, I'd be able to move back into my house. It could be about a kid going through all sorts of adventures as she learned to live alone and tried not to be so sad about her mother. I could make it look like Mom was still there too. I pictured myself moving everything back into the house and putting the books back on the bookshelves. I would make it so everything looked the way it did before, like it was supposed to. I would take all of the pictures out of the envelope and put them back in the frames in Mom's room. Then I wouldn't have to miss her so much.

I knew it could never happen, even though it was my home— my real home. It was where Mom and I were supposed to live. It wasn't fair that everything had to change when Mom died. I decided right then that I would buy the house back one day. If I stayed healthy and grew up, then nobody could stop me.

After a while I looked down at my watch and saw it was almost time for school to get out. I knew I had to start walking home. As long as I got home at the regular time, Dad and Meg wouldn't have to know that I'd skipped school. After all, the teachers don't usually take roll at the beginning of class, so I doubted they had noticed I was missing. But if I was late getting home, Meg might get all worked up and call the school, and then I would get in trouble.

I stood up and made myself leave Mom's house. But I thought maybe I would go back later that week.

Meg was waiting for me when I got home. I saw her face peering out the window by the front door, and by the time I made it up the walkway, she was outside trying to hug me. "Where were you? We were worried sick!"

"I'm fine," I said.

"But where have you been? The school called and said you were missing. Your dad just came home so he could go out to look for you."

"I just needed some time to myself so I went for a walk," I told her.

"You should've called us," she said. "We were calling and calling you. I even tried text-messaging you. Isn't that what kids do these days? I thought you'd read it and write us back."

"My phone was off," I said. "We have to turn our cell phones off when we're in school or they get taken away." Meg looked at me like she was about to say something else. "I'm gonna go up to my room," I said.

"All right," she said. She patted me on the arm as I moved past her. "I'll call Bryan and let him know you're home."

I was sitting on my bed when Dad came into my room a little while later. "Emerson Louise Price," he said. His voice was incredibly low. He didn't even sound like himself. "What do you have to say for yourself?"

"Hi, Dad," I said.

"'Hi, Dad?' Are you kidding me?" he asked. "You've really

got to be kidding me! What's gotten into you? You skipped school and ran off."

"I didn't run off," I said. "I took a walk."

"That's unacceptable," he said. Meg walked into the room behind him, but Dad just kept talking. "There isn't a double standard for you. You are not allowed to take a walk when you're supposed to be at school. You are not allowed to disappear and not call us." He turned around to look at Meg, like it was two against one, and then turned back toward me. "I just drove all over the neighborhood looking for you."

If he was driving all over the neighborhood, how come he didn't drive by Mom's house? How hard would it really have been to figure out where I wanted to be? Of course I didn't tell him any of that. "Sorry," I said.

"Sorry is not good enough, Emerson," Dad said. "I know you've been through a lot, but there are rules in this house. You can't just miss school. You're in seventh grade and your school-work is important." I hated that Dad was so obsessed with school. What did it matter? Mom was dead and I might die. And even if I didn't die, I wouldn't have a normal kind of life. Why should school matter to me at all? But of course Dad didn't understand any of that. He just kept lecturing me. "What you did today showed an absolute disrespect for school," he said, "not to mention me and Meg. Meg is pregnant—with your little sister. You cannot worry her like that."

"Bryan, it's okay," Meg said. "She just needed some time." She smiled at me. I knew it wasn't that she really understood. She was just trying to get me to like her, but it wasn't working. "I think Emmy knows enough not to do this again, right?"

"Yeah," I said.

Dad sighed really loudly. It reminded me of something I heard Lisa tell Mom once, that men are really dramatic. "All right," Dad said. He ran his fingers through his hair so it stood up a little. "I'm going downstairs to finish some work. This cannot happen again."

"Fine," I said. "I know."

They left me alone in my room. Later on Meg called me downstairs for dinner. I wasn't hungry but Dad said I had to sit at the table with them and eat something so I'd be able to take my pills. I pushed the food around on my plate and tried to make it look like I was eating. I took little bites and chewed for an extra-long time.

The next day I went back to school. Nicole seemed to be watching me carefully, like I could blow up any second and she was afraid to get too close. At lunch I went to Ms. Taylor's office to get my pills. It was another sunny day, but Nicole didn't say anything about eating outside. She didn't even tell me she'd see me in the cafeteria or that she'd save me a seat. I swallowed the three pills—big enough that they seemed like they should be medication for horses, not for people. I felt myself almost start to gag, but I swallowed again hard. "All set?" Ms. Taylor asked, and I nodded.

I walked out of her office and down the hall. My head felt light and dizzy. I blinked to make it go away. I tried to make myself feel normal. I didn't want to go back to Ms. Taylor's office and tell her I didn't feel well. I hated being sick at school. I was never the good kind of sick, like when you have appendicitis and the whole class makes you cards, or you break a bone and everyone wants to sign your cast. Whenever I didn't feel well, people thought it meant I was dying, even if the stupid truth was just that I hadn't had breakfast. I stopped for a second and put my hand on the wall. Sometimes I felt like I was outside my body, watching myself. *My life is a movie*, I thought. Then I blacked out.

Chapter 7

I don't remember being brought back to Ms. Taylor's office, but that's where I woke up. I was lying on the cot in the back, and she was right next to me, saying my name over and over again. At first it was like hearing her voice through fog, but then it got clearer and clearer, and I opened my eyes. "That's it, Emmy," she said. "You took a little fall."

"Oh," I said. The side of my head felt funny. I reached up to touch it.

"I think you're going to have a little bruise there," Ms. Taylor said. "Do you remember what happened?"

"I felt dizzy," I said.

"You fainted," she told me. "Did you eat breakfast this morning?"

"Sort of," I said. Actually I had only had a couple bites of cereal, and I hadn't really had anything to eat since breakfast the day before. There was that lousy apple and just a little bit of bagel when I had picnicked with Nicole, and then I wasn't really hungry for dinner.

"You're taking some pretty strong medication, Emmy," Ms. Taylor said. "It's important that you eat well."

"I know," I said.

"I have some saltines here," she said. She pulled open a drawer and handed me a box of crackers. "I'll call your dad and see about getting you picked up."

"I'm okay," I said.

"I'm sure you are," Ms. Taylor said. "But your dad may want to take you to the doctor just in case."

A little while later, Meg came to pick me up. Dad had been in a meeting, but Meg said it was no problem to come and get me since she worked from home and made her own schedule. She took me straight to Dr. Green's office. The receptionist, Gina, said the doctor would be with us in a few minutes. "Thanks," Meg said. She sat down on the chair across from me while we waited. She didn't say anything about it being any kind of inconvenience that I'd interrupted her in the middle of the day, or that I really should've taken better care of myself and had more for breakfast.

I watched her sitting there—her stomach was so big. She kind of looked like this ceramic Buddha that Mom used to have. Mom said it was lucky to rub his belly. Part of me wanted to rub Meg's belly, but of course I didn't. Meg rested a magazine on top of her middle and flipped the pages. Finally, Dr. Green was ready for me. I followed the nurse into one of the back rooms. Dr. Green examined me and took some blood, and then he said exactly what I already knew—I'd fainted because I hadn't eaten enough. He gave me a pamphlet about nutrition and told me to go home and take it easy.

Meg called Dad from the car and told him everything that Dr. Green had said. I hated that the doctor had given her all that information about me. It didn't really seem like any of her business. But Meg went on and on about how I was fine, and how relieved she was. Then she held out the phone to me. "Do you want to talk to your dad?"

"No," I said. She had already told him everything anyway. There wasn't anything left for me to say.

When we got back to the house, I went into the den to watch TV. Meg went upstairs and brought me the little throw blanket I kept at the end of my bed. It was from Mom's house. I used to call it my "blankey," and I still slept with it every night. I spread out on the couch, and Meg tucked the blanket around my legs, like I was a little kid and couldn't do it by myself. "All set?" she asked, and I nodded.

"So," Meg said. "I'm sort of embarrassed to tell you this, but I have today's episode of *All My Children* on the DVR. Have you ever seen it?"

"Isn't it a soap opera?"

"Yes," Meg said. "But in my defense, it's the only one I've ever watched."

I thought I remembered Mom talking about *All My Children* a couple of times. Soap operas were hardly Mom's kind of thing. She didn't really like TV that much. She said it was a waste of time. But I happened to know that Mom had watched *All My Children* every so often. It was the show she and Lisa had watched when they were in college. Mom said college was the best time of her life, and besides, she liked the clothing that one of the characters wore. Clothing was one of Mom's things. When she was a kid, she wanted to grow up to be a fashion designer. It didn't work out that way. She worked in a store, and then I was born. And then she got sick. But she still really loved fabrics and patterns, and she never said shopping was a waste of time. "I don't really like soap operas," I told Meg.

"Oh," Meg said. "I really shouldn't watch them either. I should be a better reader, like you are."

I knew I had hurt her feelings, and I felt kind of bad. It was a weird feeling, since I wasn't used to feeling bad when it came to Meg. I didn't think I should, because it wasn't fair to Mom. Then again, being nice isn't the same thing as liking someone. Mom wanted me to be a nice person. It was so hard to figure out. I kind of felt light-headed. "It's just that the soap operas are always on when I'm in school, so I never get to watch them," I said.

"Of course," Meg said. "Well, do you want to watch it with me now? I could tell you what's going on while we watch."

I shrugged. "I guess," I said.

"Great," Meg said. "Let me just fix you a snack first." She went to the kitchen and came back a few minutes later with a towel and a tray. I sat up a little. Meg spread the towel on my blanket to protect it from crumbs, and put the tray on top. "Is there anything else you need?" she asked.

I looked down at the tray—she'd given me some of the whole wheat pasta dish left over from the night before, a small bowl of fruit salad, and a couple of cookies. There was a glass of water and also some milk for the cookies. "No, this is fine," I said.

It was nice to be home sick, but not really sick. It was certainly better than being at school. Meg turned on the TV, clicked through the list of things saved on the DVR until she got to *All My Children*, and hit Play. I wondered if I should make room for her on the couch, but she sat in one of the side chairs instead. You can't see the TV quite as well from the chairs, but she didn't complain.

Even though I'd never watched the show before, it wasn't really hard to figure out what was going on. Plus, every so often, Meg would tell me something she thought I should know, like, "That's Krystal, and she's in love with Adam, even though he tried to kidnap her baby," or "Tad has come back from the dead a couple of times." I tried to figure out who the person was whose clothes Mom liked, but I couldn't tell. Most of the women on the show were really stylish. I looked to see if one of the stylish women was wearing red—Mom's favorite color. But the outfits seemed to be every color but red. It could've been any one of them. For a second—just one little second—I thought, *I'll have to ask Mom which one it is.* But then I remembered it was impossible to ask Mom anything. I hated that there was something about Mom that I couldn't figure out, that I'd never be able to ask her.

When the show ended, Meg said she was going to run to the market to pick up something for dinner. "Is there anything in particular that you want?" she asked.

"I don't know," I said.

"How about something with some iron in it then, some kind of fish?"

"I don't really like fish."

"All right," she said, "then how about some meat?"

"Okay," I said.

After Meg left, I went upstairs to my room to lie down. I closed my eyes, but I couldn't fall asleep. I heard Meg come back from the market. The car pulled into the driveway and then the door opened and slammed shut. I thought I should probably go downstairs and help her with the bags. If Meg were Mom, I would definitely go downstairs to help. But if she were Mom, everything would be different anyway. I wouldn't have been home because I wouldn't have fainted in school. I would've been eating like a regular person. I sat up in bed, trying to decide what to do. The front door opened and closed. I heard Meg's footsteps downstairs in the foyer. Then the phone rang. I answered it so I wouldn't have to make a decision about helping Meg. "Hello?" I said.

"Hey, it's Nicole."

"Hi," I said. I was surprised Nicole was calling since I had been so mean to her the day before. Maybe she felt like she had to call. That's why it's so weird to be friends with someone like me. She couldn't just stay mad and wait for me to apologize. She had to worry about me and suck it all up, because I was infected with a terrible disease. It all seemed so stupid.

"How are you?" Nicole asked.

"I'm fine," I said.

"What happened?"

"Nothing really," I said.

"I heard you fainted," Nicole said. "I was really scared."

"I'm sorry," I said, even though I wasn't sure what I was apologizing for—for being so awful at lunch or for having this disease and making her worry about me, making it so we couldn't be normal.

"That's okay," she said. "I'm glad you're okay."

"Who told you about it?"

"Rachel said Andy Maxwell saw you just fall down in the hall," Nicole said. "He's the one who called Ms. Taylor."

"Oh," I said.

"As soon as I heard about it, I went to Ms. Taylor's office," Nicole continued. "But you were already gone and she wouldn't tell me anything."

I couldn't believe Ms. Taylor actually believed in protecting my privacy. "It wasn't a big deal anyway," I said. "I just didn't eat enough."

"Are you coming to school tomorrow?"

"I don't know," I said. "I guess I am. There isn't really anything wrong with me." Well, there wasn't anything wrong with me besides being infected with the same disease that killed Mom, but I didn't say that to Nicole.

"Good," she said. "So, do you need your homework assignments or anything?"

"Not really. I think since I fainted they probably won't expect me to do them."

Nicole laughed. "Probably not," she said.

I didn't really feel like being on the phone anymore, so I told Nicole I had to go help Meg with dinner. But when I hung up, I just settled back into bed. Dad came home on the early side. He came straight up to my room to check on me. I pretended that he'd woken me up when he opened the door, but really I'd just been lying there. "Feeling better?" he asked.

"Yeah," I said.

"Good," he said. "Meg's whipping up quite a dinner downstairs."

Dad was right—a little while later when I went down to dinner, I saw Meg had made a big to-do out of the whole thing, like it was someone's birthday or something. She had set up the nice dishes, and there was a big salad and a steak with some sort of sauce on top. Dad pushed his salad aside and went right for the steak. I watched as he stabbed the meat with his fork and cut into it. He took a bite and closed his eyes while he chewed. He made a sound like it was so good, he just couldn't take it. "Mmm-mmm," he said. "You should make red meat more often, Meg."

"It's not good for you to eat it too often," Meg said.

"But it is so excellent," Dad said. "You've got to try this, Emmy Lou."

I dipped the edge of my fork into the sauce and tasted it. It was kind of garlicky and kind of peppery, but also creamy. It was like paste with flecks floating in it. "The sauce is weird," I said.

"Oh no," Meg said. "I knew I should have put it on the side. Do you want me to make you something else?"

Right then I knew I could say anything and get away with it because they were worried about me. I could make a big deal about the sauce and tell Meg I wanted a whole other meal, and she would give it to me. It was just like how Nicole magically wasn't mad at me. For the longest time, I hadn't wanted people to treat me differently because of AIDS, but being sick had its advantages too. The thing is, Mom would've seen right through me. She would've told me to knock it off and eat what was on my plate. "No, it's okay," I told Meg. "I can just scrape it off a little."

After dinner, Dad and Meg told me I didn't have to help clean up, so I went up to my room, and the next day I went back to school, just like I told Nicole I would. At lunchtime I walked down the hall to Ms. Taylor's office. I definitely felt better than I had the day before. I'm sure it was because I'd had all that steak for dinner, and Meg had made me an omelet for breakfast also. Even so, I just didn't feel like taking my pills.

I wondered what would really happen if I didn't take them this one time. Probably nothing. The doctors say if you miss a dose or take your pills at different times, you can build up immunities and the medication will stop working. But what were the chances of that happening if I just missed it this once? And what would happen if I stopped taking them altogether? I tried to think of the absolute worst thing that could happen—I could get really sick and die—and I felt my heart start to beat faster. I was scared, but it was something else, too. I sort of felt excited. If I stopped taking my pills and I got sick, Dad and Meg would take care of me like they had the night before. I wouldn't have to worry about being in school and having people look at me knowing that I was so different from everyone else. I could just sit in the den and be someone who watched soap operas in the middle of the day. And if I died, maybe I'd get to see Mom. I wouldn't have to miss her anymore. All the other stuff—like boys, and being alone forever—wouldn't matter. I turned around, away from Ms. Taylor's office and went to the cafeteria instead.

I sat next to Nicole just like it was any other day. I pretended like everything was the same, but I wondered if it would start to feel different. I don't think I had ever missed a dose of my medication before, so I wasn't sure what to expect. After lunch I had math. Our teacher, Mr. Watkins, was writing something on the board when Ms. Taylor pushed open the door. Mr. Watkins turned around when he heard the door open. "I'm sorry to disturb you," Ms. Taylor said. "I just need to borrow Emerson for a few minutes."

"Of course," Mr. Watkins said. I got up and tried not to look at anyone as I made my way down the aisle to the door. I knew everyone was looking at me. They all knew I had fainted the day before, and they probably thought it meant I was really sick since Ms. Taylor was tracking me down in class. Out in the hallway, I told Ms. Taylor that I had been distracted during lunch and I'd forgotten to go to her office to take my pills. She looked at me like she didn't really believe me, but she didn't say anything about it. She just handed me my pills and a cup of water.

The rest of the day went by slowly, and I couldn't wait to be home. But when I got there, Dad's car was in the driveway. As I was walking up the steps to the house, the front door opened. Dad stood in the doorway. He was still in his work clothes, but his tie was loosened and the top button of his shirt was undone. I wished I could turn around and go back to school. I wished

I could turn around and make time go backward. It would be amazing if time were really like a place, and if you walked back to where you had been before, you could actually go back in time. I stopped for a second on the steps, just thinking about it. I was trying to think of what exact time I wanted to go back to the most. "Come inside, Emerson," Dad said. "We have a lot to talk about."

I followed Dad inside. Meg was waiting for us in the living room. Dad sat next to her on the couch and motioned for me to sit down on the chair across from them. It was like there was an invisible line separating us. I was on one side, and they were on another, like we were at war. I guess Meg wasn't going to defend me this time. Dad said that Ms. Taylor had called him at work and told him that I hadn't taken my pills on time. "It's not a big deal," I said. "I forgot, so I took them a little while later."

"Not a big deal?" Dad said. I was beginning to notice that whenever he was mad at me, he repeated the last thing I'd said and tried to make it sound ridiculous. It made me want to laugh. I felt the sides of my mouth turning up just a little.

"You can wipe that grin off your face, Emerson," Dad said. "This isn't a joke. You don't just have the flu, you know. You can't forget to take your medication. You could build up resistance if you miss a dose. You know that—you've been doing this every day for nearly your entire life. This isn't like you!"

I didn't feel like laughing anymore. I wanted to tell him that he didn't know what was or wasn't like me. He hardly knew me at all.

Dad continued. "I don't know what to do," he said. "Maybe you need to see a doctor."

"I already saw the doctor," I said.

"No, I mean a psychiatrist," he said. "Someone you can talk to."

"No way," I told him.

"Well, we're going to do something about this, Emerson," he said, his voice getting louder. "This is unacceptable behavior. Do you know what your mother would say if you pulled something like this with her?"

My chest felt like it was about to explode. I stood up because I couldn't stay sitting down. He didn't have a right to talk about her. It was up to me to remember her. "Shut up," I said.

Dad ignored me. "I'll tell you what she'd say," he said.

"Shut up!" I said, and this time I shouted. "You don't know what she'd say! You left! Besides, she can't say anything, she's dead!"

I turned because I was going to run up to my room, but Dad stood up fast and grabbed my arm. He jerked me so I had to turn around and face him. "And you're alive," he said. "And you're wasting it. Do you know how hard your mother fought to live? The medication is working for you. It's a gift. You just need to take it. But you're wasting this gift you have."

Dad didn't know what he was talking about. My life was the opposite of a gift. Mom was dead and it was so unfair, so why should I have to appreciate life and want to live? My life was so much worse than everyone else's. Why should I have to take my pills?

It was all just too much. I felt like I was fighting with everyone. People were either mad at me or they felt sorry for me so they couldn't be mad at me. It's not like I wanted to be that way, but I didn't know how to be any other way. When Mom was around, I had felt okay. There was someone there who understood what it felt like to be me. But without her, I didn't know if I was okay. I didn't know who I was at all. Everyone always said what a miracle it was that Dad didn't get infected when he and Mom were married, but I realized it would be easier if Dad were HIV-positive, too. It's not that I wanted him to be sick. I just didn't want to be so alone. Thinking that made me feel even more hateful.

"You're skipping school and skipping doses," Dad continued. "You're hurting yourself and I won't have it. I won't have you throw your life away. You need to think about the future, Emerson. You need to move forward."

Moving forward would be away from Mom. It was easy for him to say. He didn't even miss her. He could pretend she didn't exist.

"Your dad loves you, Emmy," Meg said. "This is all because we love you."

I looked down at her, sitting on the couch. What right did she have to be there? I couldn't believe I had ever thought about being nice to her. I hated her and I hated Dad. "You're hurting me," I said, and I moved my arm so Dad had to let go of it. Then I ran upstairs to my room without looking back.

Chapter 8

I stayed in my room all night long. I wanted to stay there forever, but Dad and Meg would never have let me. Meg knocked
on my door the next morning to tell me breakfast was ready, and
then of course I had to go back to school.

Ms. Taylor was as annoying as ever. The next Monday, I
went to the bathroom before going to take my pills. When I got
to her office she said, "I was beginning to think you had forgotten." She dragged the word forgotten out, so I knew she really
meant that she was beginning to think I had blown off taking my
medication again. Throwing away the gift I had been given, like
Dad said.

Ms. Taylor doled my pills out and watched me swallow
them. "I'll see you tomorrow, Emmy, okay?" she said.

It's not like I had a choice. "Yeah," I said.

I was supposed to visit Lisa that weekend, and I was afraid
Dad would change his mind because of everything that had
happened. I was all prepared to have a fight with him about it.

But when Lisa called to check in, Dad got on the phone and told her that he and Meg would drive me into Manhattan on Saturday. They were going to stay in the city for the day and go to some deli that Meg had read about that supposedly had the best pickles in the world. She said she was craving pickles because she was pregnant. Dad and Meg would drive home on Saturday night, and Lisa and her husband Grant would drive me back to Connecticut on Sunday.

I got on the phone with Lisa after Dad was done talking to her. "So your dad's coming to New York for pickles," Lisa said.

"I don't really care what they're gonna eat, since I don't have to be with them," I told her.

"Well," she said, "Grant said he would be in charge of entertaining Oliver all day on Saturday, so it's just you and me." Oliver was Lisa's son. He was just a year old. I'd met him only a couple of times. He was cute, but I was still glad to have Lisa to myself. "Is there anything in particular you want to do?"

"I don't know," I said. "I'm just really excited to come."

"I'm excited too," Lisa said. "I'll think of something special for us."

On Saturday morning, Dad, Meg, and I pulled up in front of Lisa's building. I had called Lisa on the way, so she was in the lobby waiting for me. She ran outside as soon as she saw me getting out of the car. "Hey, sweetheart," she said. She grabbed my hands and pulled me to her. I hugged her back. I felt like crying, but I didn't want to in front of Dad and Meg. It just seemed like forever since I'd seen Lisa.

Meg stayed in the car, but Dad got out to get my bag from the trunk and say hello to Lisa. I could tell Lisa didn't really want to see him. She didn't hug him hello like she hugged me. Dad put his arm around me and kissed the top of my head. With

Lisa standing next to me, I felt the way I had at Mom's funeral—like I belonged with Lisa more than with Dad.

"Got everything you need?" Dad asked.

"Yeah," I said.

"Make sure you come home early enough tomorrow so you can do your homework," he said.

"I brought it with me," I told him. I hadn't really, but I had my backpack, so Dad would never know.

"Okay, Emmy Lou," he said. "Ciao." It was one of his things—saying hello or good-bye in another language. I thought it was incredibly dumb. Meg waved to me from the car.

Lisa and I took the elevator up to her apartment so I could drop off my stuff. When we walked in the door, the baby crawled up to her and she scooped him up. "Hey, Ollie-boy," Lisa said. "Say hi to Emmy." Oliver opened and closed his hand into a little fist. "Good waving," Lisa told him. He twisted in her arms and reached down to let her know he wanted to be put back on the floor. I watched him crawl toward a toy truck.

Grant came into the room and hugged me hello. He told Lisa and me that we should get out and enjoy our day. "Oliver and I are going to watch some football and drink some beer," he said.

"What?" I asked.

"Oh, you can't ever believe anything he says," Lisa said. "He's just kidding."

"I am not," Grant said. "Oliver loves football and beer. Come on, Ollie, we gotta put on your lucky socks. We'll tailgate in the living room."

"This is our cue to leave," Lisa told me. She grabbed her purse and we went back out to the hall to wait for the elevator. When we got downstairs the doorman asked Lisa if he could get us a cab, but Lisa said we were going to walk. "Thanks anyway," Lisa said.

"Have a good day, Mrs. Palladino," the doorman said.

"Where are we going?" I asked.

"You'll see," Lisa said. I followed her as we turned the corner and headed downtown. "God, it's so nice out. I love the weather like this. Doesn't the city just look beautiful?"

I hadn't ever thought of Manhattan as beautiful before. I always just thought of it as crowded, with a lot of buildings and not a lot of trees. But I guess it was beautiful in its own way. The buildings were shiny, and I liked how the mannequins were all dressed up in the store windows. "Do you remember the name of the woman on *All My Children* who my mom thought had the best clothes?" I asked.

"Yup," Lisa said. "That was Erica Kane." I loved how Lisa just knew things about Mom. "What made you think of that?" she asked.

"Meg watches *All My Children*," I said.

"Oh," Lisa said. "How is it, living with your dad and Meg?"

I shrugged. "I don't know," I said. "Sometimes it's like I barely know them. It's been so long since I've lived with my dad."

"Yeah, well, I don't know what Bryan was thinking when he left your mom and married Meg," Lisa said. "But hey, we can make this day totally free of the two of them. Today it's just us. What do you think?"

"I think that sounds great," I said.

"Good," Lisa said. She pointed down the block. "See that bright red door?"

"Yeah," I said.

"That's where we're going."

There was a doorman standing in front of the building with the red door. I think it's funny how in Manhattan there are people whose job it is to open doors, as though Lisa and I couldn't do it by ourselves. This doorman even wore a top hat, which made me want to laugh. Lisa seemed to think the whole thing was perfectly normal. "Have a good day, ladies," the man said.

"Thank you," Lisa said. "We will."

We walked inside. The lobby smelled like perfume. "Welcome to the Red Door Salon and Spa," a woman said. "Are you checking in?"

"Yes, I have a reservation for two under Palladino," Lisa said.

"You're on the sixth floor," the woman said. "The elevators are straight in the back."

"What is this place?" I asked Lisa as we got into the elevator.

"It's Elizabeth Arden," Lisa said. "Haven't you ever heard of it?" I shook my head. "It's a day spa," she told me.

"Are we eating here?" I asked.

"No, of course not," Lisa said.

"Then how come we have a reservation?"

"For our hair and nails," she told me.

We got upstairs and a woman came up to greet us. "Hello, ladies," she said. "Can I get you something to drink?"

"I'd love some water," Lisa said.

"Of course," the woman said. She turned to me. "And for you?"

"Water, please," I said.

I sat next to Lisa on a bright red leather couch. The woman came back and brought us water with little apple slices floating in the glasses. She also handed us magazines to read while we waited, and told us to let her know if we needed anything else. "She's acting like we're famous," I whispered to Lisa.

"It's what they do here," Lisa said.

"Oh," I said. I knew it was cool to be treated like we were

famous, but I felt like the day spa probably cost too much money.

Lisa must have noticed that I looked uncomfortable. "Em, it's okay," she said. "It's been a tough year. I think we deserve to be pampered and have a day of beauty, don't you?"

For a second I thought about how Meg had kind of pampered me that day she brought me a snack on a tray when I didn't feel well. But then I remembered it was supposed to be a day free of Dad and Meg. I looked over at Lisa. I decided to just enjoy the day. "Okay," I said. I sat back on the red couch and tasted the water. There was just the slightest hint of apple in it, which made me a little hungry. I wanted to reach into the water and fish out one of the apple slices to eat it. I turned the glass slightly to see if one of the slices would just pop up on top so I could get it easily. The day spa didn't seem like the kind of place where you were supposed to dip your fingers into your glass.

Someone called our names, and I put down my water and followed Lisa to another part of the room, where we each got our own bright red chair. A woman named Monica came up behind me and started playing with my hair. She held it up like in a bun, and then let it fall back down to my shoulders. "So what do you want to do with this today?" she asked.

"I'm not sure," I told her.

"Well," Monica said. "Let's get you washed up, and then we can blow you out and decide how to style it."

"Okay," I said. Monica brought me over to the sinks, even though I had just washed my hair that morning. I sat down in one of those special seats for getting your hair washed, where there's a little cutout at the top of the chair so you can tilt your head back into the sink. Monica spent an extra long time washing my hair. It must have been twenty minutes, and her fingers rubbed harder and harder into my scalp. Finally she turned the faucet on and rinsed out my hair, which also took a really long time. She told me she was going to give me a conditioning treatment, so my hair would be strong and shiny. "This stuff is amazing," she said. "We give it to all the celebrities who come in here."

"Okay," I said.

Afterward, Monica brought me back to my red leather chair and blew out my hair with about five different big round brushes. I looked up at her in the mirror. It was amazing how she could hold them all and the blow dryer. Monica pressed down on my head to position me so she could use another round brush. There were brushes sticking out all over my head. She suggested a bunch of different ways to do my hair, but I couldn't decide. Finally I asked her if she could French braid it, because Mom used to braid my hair. Monica separated my hair into sections and braided my hair slowly, so every strand was perfectly smooth. Everything at Elizabeth Arden took a really long time.

When my hair was finished, I was brought over to another part of the salon to have my nails done. Lisa was already there. She had also had her hair blown out, but it was just down on her shoulders. I wondered how much she was paying to have her hair look exactly the same as it always did.

The manicurist told me her name was Pia, and she asked me what color I wanted my nails painted. I pointed to the color Lisa had picked out. Pia sat down at my feet. I picked up a magazine and pretended to read it as Pia washed my feet, and then put them in little slippers so she could paint my toenails. Someone else came over to give me a manicure at the same time. The woman who had done Lisa's nails took Lisa's credit card out of her purse for her so Lisa wouldn't ruin her nails when she had to pay. A few minutes later, the woman came back and put the credit card back in Lisa's bag. When it was all done, Lisa and I sat on a bench in our slippers, waiting for our nails to dry. We put our hands and feet into little air blowers to make the drying go faster.

"Do you want to get your makeup done too?" Lisa asked.

"No, it's okay," I said. I didn't want her to have to spend any more money. Besides, it was hard to really talk to Lisa when we were in the day spa.

Lisa pulled her hands out of the air blower and touched one of her fingernails lightly. "Well, I think these are done," she said. "Ready to go?"

I pulled out my hands and rubbed my finger along the polish on my thumbnail. It was completely smooth. "Yeah, I'm ready," I said.

On our way out, Lisa ran into someone she knew from Oliver's playgroup. They hugged each other like they were best friends, but afterward Lisa whispered that she didn't really like her. "She's nuts," Lisa said. "She read some article in the *Times* about potty-training kids when they're three months old, and she's really doing it. She takes the baby into the bathroom a hundred times a day. She does it while we're in playgroup. Can you imagine?"

"No," I said, but I did try and imagine it. Even though I didn't know exactly how old babies were when they were potty-trained, I knew three months was definitely too young. They were still so small. They would probably fall in the toilet. I started to laugh. Lisa took my hand and pulled me out of the spa.

We walked back to her apartment and stopped at a bunch of places on the way. We went into one store because Lisa wanted to try on a dress that was in the window. It was so beautiful, but they didn't have Lisa's size. She did end up buying me a shirt.

Even though I told her she really didn't have to get me anything, I was secretly glad that she did. I loved shopping with Lisa, and it was nice to have something to remember the day. "I used to do this with Simone," Lisa said as she handed me the bag. "When I was still single and I was worried about what to wear on dates, she would come into New York to help me shop. She picked out my outfit for my first date with Grant."

"Mom took me shopping a lot too," I said.

"I can tell," Lisa said. "You have her fashion sense."

"Thanks," I said. My new shirt was the kind of thing Mom would have loved. The stitching was really small and precise. Mom liked things that looked like the designer had paid attention to the details.

"I think about your mom all the time," Lisa said. "She was my best friend."

"She was my best friend too," I said. It was different than being best friends with Nicole. I knew Lisa understood what I meant.

"She was amazing," Lisa said. "I remember before I met Grant, when I was worried I would never get married or have kids, Simone was there for me. She kept telling me not to waste time worrying. I thought she just didn't understand, but she was right. She was always right."

"I know," I said. It was nice not being the only one remembering Mom. It made her feel so much closer. I reached up and fingered my braid. Dad and Meg didn't matter at all.

Later on we had dinner at Lisa's apartment. Grant made pasta with red sauce, but he put the sauce on the side since Oliver wouldn't eat that part. Oliver stayed up much later than Seth and Riley. He sat with us through dinner. He started out in a highchair, but he got a little whiny, so Lisa pulled him out and let him sit on her lap. She put a little of the plain pasta on the side of her plate, and Oliver grabbed at it with his hands. His face got really greasy. I knew Meg would never let her kid eat like that. She hated mess so much. But Lisa didn't seem to care and it made me love her even more.

After dinner, we all sat on the couch in the den to watch a movie. Grant had Oliver on his lap. Oliver put his fist up to his cheek and leaned into it. It looked like he was thinking really hard about the movie, even though I was sure it wasn't anything he could understand. "He looks like that statue," I told Lisa. "You know, the one of the guy who's some sort of great thinker."

"Oh, he always does that," Lisa said. "I think his Indian name would be 'Chief Fist to His Face.'"

"Isn't he sort of young to be a chief?" I asked.

"Oh no," Lisa said. "Not my son. He was born a chief." She reached over to take Oliver off of Grant's lap, and she turned him around so he was facing me. Oliver moved his fist from his cheek to grab onto my finger. I thought about how normal it all seemed—like, I could be just visiting Lisa for the weekend. Maybe she wanted my help with the baby, or maybe she wanted company because normally she's stuck in an apartment with all boys. It felt like Mom could be home in Highlands, waiting for me. When I got back, I would tell her all about it. As long as I was at Lisa's, it almost seemed like everything was the way it was supposed to be.

"I wish I didn't have to go back tomorrow," I said.

"I wish we didn't have to take you there," Lisa said. "Bryan always rubs me the wrong way."

"Honey," Grant said.

"I'm sorry," Lisa said. She turned to me. "I know he's your father, and I know he loves you very much. I just think he made some really bad choices."

"Yeah," I said.

"That's enough, girls," Grant said. "Really."

"Oh, Grant," Lisa said, "how can you possibly expect us to take you seriously when you're wearing that shirt?" I leaned forward to look at Grant's shirt. It was just a white T-shirt. Across the front of it were the words, *What can you do with your PC? With our new ultra X7 technology, ANYTHING YOU WANT!*

"What about my shirt?" Grant asked.

"I think it might be the nerdiest shirt in the entire world," Lisa said.

"What does it mean?" I asked.

"I have no idea," Lisa said. "I doubt Grant even knows what it means."

"Of course I do," Grant said. "I'm very smart."

"Okay, Einstein, what does it mean?" Lisa asked.

"I couldn't possibly explain it to you now," Grant said. "It would take too much time."

"Grant!" Lisa said, tossing one of the throw pillows at him. She didn't say anything more about Dad. I leaned back into the couch. I wondered why Grant was defending Dad. Maybe it was because he was a father himself, or maybe he just thought I was too young to hear bad things about my parents. But I knew Lisa was right. She was Mom's best friend, after all. She must have heard all about Dad's choices.

I hated driving back to Connecticut the next day. I sat in the back, next to Oliver in his car seat. Grant was driving, and Lisa was up front next to him. Nobody talked much. We pulled up in front of Dad's house, and Lisa and Grant got out of the car to hug me good-bye. I hugged Grant quickly, but I held on to Lisa longer. "You'll come back soon," Lisa said. "Now that summer is coming, you can stay for more than just the weekend, okay?"

"Okay," I said.

Dad came out of the house to say hello. I knew he was there because I could hear him behind me, talking to Grant. Suddenly I missed Mom so much. I always missed her, but I missed her even more right then. I didn't want to let go of Lisa. I knew that when I did, I would be back in my real life.

Chapter 9

It was hard to sleep that night. It was too hot. I felt closed in, like I couldn't escape. I kicked the blankets off, but it didn't help. I was screaming in my head: *I want to go home!*

I got up to go to the bathroom. I didn't really have to go, but I flushed the toilet anyway. At Dad's house, the toilets flushed in a loud, forceful way. I once heard toilets flush differently under the equator. They flushed in a different way at Mom's house, even though we were on the same side of the equator. And Meg bought the wrong kind of toothpaste. Mom and I had always used Colgate, but Meg bought Crest.

"Mommy," I said out loud. "Mommy, please. I want to go home." I wanted her to answer me. I was just so sad and I needed her to comfort me. Losing her was the worst thing. How could I get through it without her?

I walked into my room and got back into bed. The air was humid and my hair was sticking to the back of my neck. It was still in the braid from Saturday. Monica had made the braid so perfect and tight that it had lasted all the way to Sunday. But now it felt too thick and heavy, like it was weighing my head down. The center of my back started to ache, right in the place I couldn't reach. I flipped my head so the braid would be off of my neck, but it didn't work. I sat up again and pulled the rubber band out of my hair. Mom used to undo my French braids carefully, layer by layer, so I didn't get knots. But I just wanted it all out as quickly as possible, so I pulled it hard. The braid fell out but my hair was all knotty. It felt even thicker than Nicole's hair, and I was still hot and uncomfortable. I thought I might even pass out again.

I got out of bed and walked over to the desk to get my scissors. Then I gathered all my hair up with one hand. I put the scissors around my hair and pressed down to cut it all off. It was harder to cut than I thought it would be. They always make it look so easy when I'm getting a haircut, but I guess it doesn't work as well when you have your hair in your fist and you're trying to cut it all at once. I was crying because it was taking too long. I pushed on the scissors so my fingers hurt. Finally they closed down and my hair fell to the floor. I stared at it lying there. It looked like a nest. I put the scissors back on my desk, but I left my hair there. I didn't feel like cleaning it up.

I got into bed again. The back of my neck felt empty. All of a sudden I realized I could've just turned on the air conditioner to cool off, or I could've opened the window. But the funny thing was that I really didn't care. My hair had looked pretty, but what good did being pretty really do me? It's not like it changed my life at all. It's not like it made anything better. I squeezed my eyes shut and waited to fall asleep.

Chapter 10

The next morning I came downstairs, and Dad and Meg looked at me like I was an alien. My hair was just above my shoulders, so it wasn't that short, but the bottom was all uneven. It sort of looked like I had been attacked with scissors. "What did you do?" Dad asked.

I thought it was pretty obvious what I had done. "I cut my hair," I said. "I was hot."

"That's some look," he said.

"If you want, I can make an appointment at the salon in town," Meg said. "That's where I get my hair done. They could even out the bottom for you, unless there's a place you'd rather go."

I shook my head, which felt funny. My hair slapped my chin. "No thank you," I said.

Before I left for school, I tried to figure out if there was a way to fix my hair so it didn't look so strange. It was too short to put up in a ponytail. I tucked the sides behind my ears, but the hair kept popping back out. I looked in the mirror. "Whatever," I said out loud. I tried to make myself not care, but I didn't want to go to school. I didn't want anyone to see me. I thought about crawling back into bed and telling Dad and Meg that I was too sick to leave the house.

"Emmy," Dad called. "I'm leaving now. Do you want a lift?"

I didn't want to go, but I didn't want to be home all day with Meg, either. "Fine," I said.

At least there were only a couple of weeks of school left. Nicole had been counting the days until the end of school for the past month, which is something she always did. I guess everyone does that, but Nicole made this big deal out of announcing exactly how many days were left every morning. Then she would cross out the day before in her day planner. She made a giant X in a different color every day. Nicole says she's a visual learner, so she's into things like that. She likes to see things on the page. She also always made flashcards when she had a test to study for, because she needed to see a picture or a word or something in order to be able to memorize it. I used to help her make flashcards. We would buy multicolored index cards and color code the different subjects. Then we would flip through them and test each other.

That morning there were exactly ten days left of school, and I knew Nicole would be excited about it because it was the last day in double digits. But she forgot all about the countdown when she saw me. "What happened to your hair?" she asked.

"I went to New York," I said, as if that explained it, even though I didn't even cut my hair when I was in New York.

"I didn't know you were going to New York," she said.

"I went to see Lisa," I told her.

"Oh," she said. "That's weird."

"What do you mean?" I asked.

"It's just weird that you went to New York without telling me," Nicole said.

"You go lots of places without telling me," I said.

"Like where?" she asked.

"I don't know where you're going if you don't tell me," I said.

Nicole paused for a second, just looking at me, and then she smiled. "Okay," she said. "Let's make a deal. I'll tell you if I go anywhere, and you tell me if you go anywhere."

"What if I'm going to the bathroom?" I asked. "Should I tell you first?"

"Oh, Emmy, come on," Nicole said. "I mean if you're going anywhere good, like to New York, or on vacation, or something. Definitely if you're sleeping over somewhere. Deal?"

"Yeah, it's a deal," I said.

"Cool," Nicole said. Then she started laughing and she shook her head.

"What?" I asked.

"I just can't get used to your hair," she said.

I raised my hand up and tried to tuck my hair behind my ears, but of course it didn't work. It stayed put for about five seconds and then popped out again. I wondered how long it took for hair to grow.

"So, are you coming over today to do flashcards?" Nicole asked. "You know there are only ten days left of school." We had a bunch of tests the next week because it was the end of the year. But I was so behind in my classes, and I didn't even really care about my grades anymore. The teachers might have been checking to see that I came to class every day, but no one made sure that I paid attention. Dad would've been mad if he knew, but he wasn't in class with me, so it didn't matter.

Nicole opened her backpack and pulled out a little pile of

index cards that were sort of a metallic color. We used to get the regular pastel-colored ones from the office supply store in town. "Aren't these cool?" she asked. She handed me the card off the top so I could see. They must have been for our science class, because the first card said "Conservation of Energy." I flipped it over to see what was written on the back. "Energy cannot be created or destroyed." I hadn't been paying attention at all in science, so I didn't remember Mrs. O'Hagan ever teaching us about it. But I looked at the card and pretended to be studying it. I tried to hear the words in Mom's voice. It was this thing I did to remember how she sounded. Sometimes I would try to think of actual things she had said, and sometimes I would take a snippet of something and try to think of what it would sound like in her voice. *Energy cannot be created or destroyed.* Maybe that meant that Mom wasn't actually gone.

"So?" Nicole asked.

"I can't make flashcards today," I told her, and I handed her back the card.

"Why not?" Nicole asked.

It was a weird question. People aren't supposed to ask things like that, in case the answer is something like, *Well, I just don't feel like it.* But Nicole was my best friend, so I guess she thought she was allowed. I just didn't know how to answer her. "Maybe Rachel will make flashcards with you," I said.

"Rachel's mom doesn't let her study with other people," Nicole said. "She thinks it means we'll just goof off."

I realized that meant Nicole had already asked Rachel about the flashcards. I wasn't sure if she had asked Rachel if she wanted to study with both Nicole and me, or just the two of them. I don't know why I was upset about it, since I didn't want to study with Nicole anyway. "What about Isabella or Julia?" I asked.

"I'd rather study with you than anyone else," Nicole said.

For a second it was like she could read my mind. I looked at Nicole. I tried to really see her, like see inside of her. She reached up and flipped her hair to the side. It was long enough for a pony-tail or a bun or a braid. She had the kind of hair you could do anything with. I wished I hadn't done what I did to my hair. I wished so many things.

We were staring at each other, like that game we used to play, waiting to see who would blink first. Finally, my eyes started to burn and I blinked. "Maybe you could ask Zach Andrews to help you with the flashcards," I said.

"I'm not gonna ask Zach," she said. "I barely even know him."

"Oh," I said.

"You're really not gonna come?" she asked. "It would be fun."

She was right; at least maybe she was. It definitely used to be fun, before Mom died. That's why Nicole and I were best friends—because we could have fun doing anything, even study-ing, as long as we were together. It had been that way since third grade. But now having fun felt impossible, like I didn't know how to do it anymore. I wasn't even sure Nicole still wanted to be my best friend. Maybe she just felt bad for me and was trying to be nice. I felt so messed up inside. I shook my head.

"Come on, Emmy," Nicole said. "I know you're sad, but your mom would want you to be happy."

I knew Nicole mentioned Mom because of our fight—because I told her I was always thinking about Mom. But I hated when people thought they knew what Mom would want. Nothing anyone ever said about Mom was right, and anyway, there was no way I would really be happy ever again.

"I'm pretty tired," I said.

When I got home, Meg heard me and came out into the foyer. She was wearing a T-shirt that Dad had bought her as a joke. It was bright yellow and it said *Under Construction* across her middle, like those signs that were posted up in town when the supermarket was being redone. It was so stupid. I knew Mom would never wear anything like that when she was pregnant. It wasn't fashionable at all. I wondered if Meg had left the house like that. "Hey, Emmy Lou," she said. "How was school?"

"Fine," I said.

"Do you have a lot of homework?" she asked.

I shrugged my shoulders and made a sound that was kind of like a sigh and kind of like a groan. Meg probably thought it was about school and not about her. "I don't know," I said.

"You don't know?"

"I guess so," I said. "There's a lot of reading. You know, finals are coming up." Maybe if she thought I had a bunch of stuff to read she would stop bothering me. It's not like I was actually planning on doing any schoolwork. I just wanted to be left alone.

"Of course," Meg said. "I'm just asking because I wanted to make sure you didn't want me to take you to get your hair fixed."

"I'm sure," I said. I walked back to the kitchen to get a glass of water. I would get the water, and maybe a little snack, and go up to my room until dinner.

Meg followed me into the kitchen. "Really, Emmy," she said. "I called the salon, just to see if they had room for you. Deanne—she's the woman who cuts my hair—she's just the sweetest, and she said she could squeeze you in. I like your hair this length. I think once Deanne evens the ends out, it'll look great. What do you say?"

I didn't answer. I was surprised she kept asking me. After

all, she knew how important Dad thought my homework was. I walked past the table. All of Meg's fancy dishes were laid out on it. The whole top of the table was entirely covered with dinner plates, salad plates, and little cups and saucers. "What's all this?" I asked.

"It's the china," she said. "I took it out to clean."

I knew it was because of her stupid nesting, getting ready for that baby I didn't want to ever be around. It didn't even make sense because babies don't eat off china. Meg cooked and cleaned. Maybe next she would paint the entire house. Maybe that was why she was trying to fix me. "Honey," she said, "let me take you to Deanne. You don't have to be embarrassed."

"I'm not embarrassed," I said.

"Okay," Meg said. "So let's just go."

Why couldn't she just shut up? I wanted to put my hands over my ears. I stepped back and bumped against the table. I didn't mean to, but the dishes rattled a little bit.

"Oh, honey," Meg said. "Please be careful with the china." *What a perfectionist*, I thought. I could hear the words in Mom's voice. *Just wait until she has children.* All of a sudden I wished I had bumped the table harder. I wanted to break something. I turned and picked up one of the plates. I held it up over my head, and then, just like that, I let go and it crashed down. Little pieces of china skidded across the floor. I looked down and they were everywhere.

"What are you doing?" Meg asked. Her voice was shaky. She bent down to pick up the shards. She hated when things were messy and out of place, but I loved the way it looked all smashed like that. I didn't want her to pick it up. I moved my arm and swept it back and forth across the table, and all of the china smashed onto the floor. Meg scooted backward and started crying. How ridiculous to cry over smashed dishes. It wasn't like they were people. "Stop it! Stop it!" she screamed, even though there wasn't anything left for me to break. "Please Emerson," Meg said. "Think about the baby."

"I don't care about the baby!" I yelled. Meg braced herself against the cabinet by the sink. She clutched her stomach. I could tell she was scared of me. I had made a grown woman scared. It was the weirdest thing. It made me feel powerful, even though everything else was out of control.

Chapter 11

After that, Dad and Meg barely spoke to me. If we happened to pass in the hall, Meg moved away from me, like she was afraid to touch me. Mostly I just stayed in my room. Sometimes I would think of Meg on the floor in the kitchen, surrounded by all the shards of broken china. She could have cut herself. Every time I thought about it, I had to squeeze my eyes shut so I wouldn't have to picture the blood.

A couple of days after I broke the china, I was in my room and I started to think about what it would be like if I just apologized to Meg. I knew it was horrible of me to break all those dishes, and part of me was sorry about what I did. It's not like anything was really Meg's fault. Why couldn't I just be nice? Maybe everything that happened was just punishment for me being a horrible person. It's not like I was so mean before Mom died, but maybe I just always had it in me to be that way.

I got up from my bed and walked over so I could see myself in the mirror above my dresser. I looked at myself as I mouthed the words. *I'm sorry. I'm sorry.* My mouth looked weird and contorted. I repeated the words in my head. The more you say the same words, the sillier they sound.

I wondered who decided what sounds mean what things. Who made up words? I remembered asking Dad about it, a long time ago. He said a lot of English words came from other languages, like Latin. "Maybe you'll study Latin in high school," he said. But making words out of other words was one thing. I wondered who made up Latin. Who made up the very first language, out of nothing at all? It made me think of Nicole's flashcards. *Energy cannot be created or destroyed.* I stared at myself in the mirror. I moved my lips so I was mouthing those words: *Energy cannot be created or destroyed.* Was Mom still there? Was she watching me? Had she seen me saying "sorry" over and over again?

I never thought I was the kind of person who believed in ghosts. It seemed so creepy and weird, but it had to be different if it was just your family. It's not like I was thinking of lots of ghosts. I turned away from the mirror and sat back on my bed. There were people on TV who said they could talk to ghosts. They sat in rooms with dimmed lights, closed their eyes, and said things like, "I'm feeling her now. She wants you to know that she's here." I couldn't apologize to Meg, just in case.

Later on I wanted a snack, so I had to leave my room. As I got closer to the kitchen, I could hear Dad and Meg talking. I was too far away to know exactly what they were saying, but I was sure they were talking about me.

Dad said something I couldn't hear. I stepped closer, and I heard Meg say, "But you have to go to work. You can't always be here when she gets home from school. Besides, the summer is coming."

"I know," Dad said.

"I just don't know how I can be here all day with her," Meg said.

I realized she was afraid to be in the house with me. "It'll be okay," Dad said. "I'm going to have a long talk with her."

"But Bryan," Meg said, "you *have* talked to her. It's not working. And we have a baby coming. You need to get her help. The next thing you know, it won't be broken dishes. It'll be something worse. I've heard all these stories about kids acting out and then turning to drugs."

I wondered if Dad would point out that I'd been on drugs every day for almost my entire life. But he just said, "I know, Meg. I know you're right." I wanted to scream. But if I opened my mouth, I wasn't sure what would come out—"I'm sorry!" or "I hate you!" I didn't say anything at all. I just turned around and went back to my room without eating anything.

The next day, Dad knocked on my door. "Yeah," I said. I was sitting on my bed. Dad came into my room and pulled the chair out from my desk. He turned it around so when he sat in it, so he could look at me. He was holding some papers in his hands, but I couldn't tell what they were.

"We need to change some things around here," Dad said. "I know you must want things to change too."

I shrugged. I wanted to lie down and roll over so I was facing the wall instead of him.

"Meg found out about a camp," Dad said. "It's called Camp Positive, and it's a sleepaway camp for girls who have HIV."

I hadn't ever gone away to camp before. I had asked Mom about it once, a couple of summers before, when Nicole was thinking of going away to camp. But Mom said she didn't like the idea of sending me away. "I don't want to go," I told Dad.

"Just listen first," Dad said. "Meg and I think this is a good idea. A change of scene would do you good, and you'll be around other kids who know what you're going through."

I doubted anyone could really understand what I was going through. Maybe these kids also had HIV, but they probably didn't have a father who abandoned their mother, and who was now having a baby with his new wife. "No thanks," I said.

"Well, Emerson," Dad said, "the thing is, this really isn't up for discussion. We have to do something about your behavior. I know you've been through a lot. Believe me, I know. You have so many reasons to be angry. You've had so much loss, and you're barely a teenager. But I really don't know how to help you. You're sullen and despondent. You keep fighting with me and with Meg. You keep pushing us away." I could tell by the way Dad was talking that he had practiced his speech. I wondered if he had stood in front of the mirror, like I had, and mouthed all the words.

"Camp isn't going to help anything," I told him.

"Maybe not," Dad said. "But we won't know until we try it. I hope you're wrong, but either way, I think maybe we all need some distance from each other."

"So this is because you want to get rid of me," I said. It was just like how he got rid of Mom. He moved out, and then he married Meg. And now he was sending me away. He probably wouldn't ever want me to come home. After all, he and Meg were having a new daughter, who would be healthy and perfect. What did they need me for?

I knew I couldn't trust Dad. He had told me at Mom's funeral that he would always be there for me, but I knew he was lying.

"Mom would never have sent me away," I said.

"Emmy, don't be like that. Camp is only for six weeks."

"Why don't I just spend the summer with Lisa?" I asked.

Dad shook his head. "You can't spend six weeks with the Palladinos," he said.

"Why not? She wants me," I told him. "She told me so. She said now that summer is coming up, she wants me to stay longer than just a weekend."

"There's a big difference between a weekend and six weeks," Dad said.

"So I'll ask her," I said.

"Emerson, the answer is no," Dad said. "The last time you came home from Lisa's, you broke the china."

"I won't do it again," I said.

"No," Dad said again. "You may not go to Lisa's."

"Then what about Aunt Laura and Uncle Rob?" I asked. "They said I was always welcome there."

"Emmy," Dad said, "you're not going to Colorado either. I've put a lot of thought into this. I really think this camp will be the best place for you."

I felt the sharpness behind my eyes. It wasn't fair. Why was everything always so unfair? I couldn't imagine anyone else I knew having their mom die and then being sent away. If Dad wanted to send me away, then fine. I didn't need him anyway. But why couldn't I live with Lisa or Aunt Laura? Why couldn't I have a say at all? Everything was so completely out of control. I should get to decide things in my own life.

All of sudden I realized that I just couldn't go to camp. If energy wasn't destroyed and there really were ghosts, then Mom might be out there. Maybe she'd still be able to find me if I was at Lisa's or Aunt Laura's. But if I went to a camp she'd never heard of, she wouldn't know where to find me. I knew it was dumb. It was the stupidest thing in the world. Dad would never understand, even if I tried to explain it to him. A tear moved down my cheek. It was hot, and it felt like it was cutting into my skin like a knife.

"Honey, don't cry. It's all going to be okay."

"Please," I said. "Don't make me go." It was so weird to be begging Dad to let me stay. I didn't even like living with him and Meg. But I didn't want to be sent away even more. I felt like one of those people who has multiple personalities. Ever since Mom died, my feelings were so mixed up about everything. Now part of me hated Dad and Meg, but part of me just wanted Dad to tell me they would never send me away.

Dad got up from the chair and came to sit with me on the bed. He touched my legs so I would move over. I pulled them up tightly against my chest. "This is for your own good," Dad said.

"You're wrong," I said. "It won't do me any good. Lisa told me you make bad choices." I wiped my face with my hands. Dad reached across me to get the box of tissues from the table beside my bed. He handed me one and I wiped my face. It felt so sticky and gross. I hated myself. I wished I were anyone but me.

"Lisa doesn't know everything about this family," Dad said.

"She knows about me," I told him. "She knows a lot more about me than you do. I don't even have anything to wear at camp." I knew I sounded stupid, but I couldn't think of anything else to say.

"We still have a couple of weeks before camp starts," Dad said. "You have your appointment with Dr. Green for your blood work, and then we'll get you whatever clothes you need, okay?" I didn't answer. Dad held up the papers he had in his hand. "Look at this," he said. "It's the brochure from the camp. It doesn't look so bad. And I have a questionnaire for you to fill out so you can let them know what you're interested in and which activities you want to do."

"I'm not interested in anything," I said.

"Just give it a chance, Emmy," Dad said. "We can fill it out together."

"You do it," I said. "I don't care what you pick."

"Emmy," Dad said, but I turned away from him. It was a joke that Dad would be picking out activities for me. He didn't know me at all.

Dad said he would be downstairs if I wanted to talk. He stood up from the bed, and the mattress lifted up just a little bit. I looked down at where he had been sitting. He had left the camp brochure next to me. There was picture of a group of kids on the front of it. They were all smiling, like they loved being there. They were probably brainwashed. If Meg picked it out, it was probably some sort of stupid health camp. They would probably make us eat organic roots and vegetables all summer long. I crumpled the brochure up in my hand and threw it away.

Chapter 12

School ended and my report card came. Amazingly, my grades weren't bad at all. At first I thought maybe there had been some kind of mix-up, and I felt really sorry for whoever accidentally got my grades. But then Dad showed me the letter that had come from the principal. Mr. Jennings had written that my final tests didn't count in my report card, because he understood I'd been through a lot in the last couple of months. He said he hoped I had a good summer and came back ready for school. Dad and Meg took the note as a sign that they were definitely right about sending me away. "You need to get away so you can come back and get a fresh start," Dad said.

There was a bus going up to camp, but Dad said he and Meg would drive me if I wanted. "Whatever," I said.

"Emmy," Dad said, "I know this is hard on you, but I want you to get as much as you can out of this. Can't you try just a little bit?"

I shook my head. I was in my room, as usual. Dad was

standing in the doorway. He lifted his hand to scratch his cheek, which is what he did sometimes at the end of the day, when he started to get his five o'clock shadow. That's what Mom used to call it when his beard started to grow in. In the mornings Dad always shaved his face, and his skin was really smooth. But at night his cheeks got scruffy again. I remembered how he would come in to kiss me good night when I was little, and I got mad when the scruff on his face scratched my cheek. I told him he should shave at night, too.

Back then I loved to watch Dad shave. He would let me sit up on the sink and hand me the razor so I could rinse it off under the faucet. Sometimes he put shaving cream on my face too. It felt so cool on my cheeks. Dad would call me Marshmallow. I would bend my finger and pretend it was a razor and move it down the sides of my face, making tracks through the shaving cream.

It all seemed like so long ago. I felt like a completely different person.

"Come on, Em," Dad said. "Talk to me. Do you want me to help you pack?"

"No," I said. "I just want some privacy. Can you leave, please?"

Dad sighed and left my room. I leaned back on my bed and listened to his footsteps as he went down the hall. They got softer and softer until I couldn't hear them anymore.

I looked across the room. Dad had brought one of the big suitcases up from the basement so I could pack my new clothes. It had been so weird to go shopping with Dad instead of Mom. He'd brought along a list he'd made of things he thought I would need at camp, kind of like a list you'd make to go to the grocery store. That's not the way Mom and I shopped for clothes. I hadn't even taken my new clothes out of the shopping bags. They were just sitting there in my room, next to the suitcase. Meg had also brought in sheets and towels, along with a toiletries bag full of shampoo and conditioner and stuff like that in it. The towels and sheets were folded up so tight, just like at a hotel. It was annoying how she could make things so neat. I got out of bed and tossed them into the suitcase, and they unfolded a little bit. I took my clothing out of the shopping bags and dumped it all in, and then I threw the toiletries bag in on top of the rest. I looked down and surveyed my work. It was messy, but it's not like it mattered.

I sat back down on my bed. *My bed,* I thought. *MY bed.* My bed, my books, my pictures, my stuff, my room. It would be here, and I would be sent away. What if Meg started wandering around, nesting and cleaning, and came into my room? I could just imagine her touching my things, dusting the shelves, rearranging stuff so it looked the way she thought it should. I opened the drawer on the table next to my bed and took out the envelope of pictures to take with me. That way, even if Meg snooped around, she wouldn't get to look at Mom's pictures. But then I thought of something else. What if Meg decided she really should be reading instead of watching *All My Children,* and she came into my room and picked up one of Mom's books? I didn't want her reading anything that belonged to Mom, or anything that Mom had picked out especially for me. I didn't want her touching them, because Mom had touched them, and that meant there was still part of Mom on them.

I got out of bed and took a pile of books off my shelf. I didn't have enough room in my suitcase to bring *all* of Mom's books, but at least I could take her favorites. I picked the ones that had bindings that were the most bent up and ragged, because I knew those were the ones she liked best—the ones she had read over and over again, and then I chose a few of the books Mom had given Lisa to give to me. It would be good to have them all at camp. I didn't think I would really talk to anyone, so at least I could read Mom's books. I stacked them as neatly as I could in a corner of the suitcase, and I put the envelope of pictures on top. Then I zipped it all up.

We left for camp the next day. It was a Sunday. I didn't say good-bye to Nicole. I knew she would be mad because I hadn't even told her I was going, but I didn't feel like talking about it. I didn't feel like talking to anyone.

Dad drove, and Meg sat in the passenger seat next to him. I was in the back. Meg is the kind of person who likes to fill up space, so she talked the whole ride up, like she thought we cared about every single thing that popped into her head. I wished I could close my ears the way I could close my eyes. Even if I put my hands over my ears, I would still hear her. We drove up the highway through the country and the road got really twisty. Meg said there were probably a lot of antique stores in the area, and Dad said maybe they would check out the antique stores on their way home. Their way home without me, of course. I hated listening to them.

"You know what I haven't had in ages?" Meg asked.

I didn't know if the question was meant for Dad or me, but I didn't answer her. "What?" Dad asked.

"A Funyun," Meg said.

"I have no idea what that is," Dad said.

"It's a cross between a Cheeto and an onion ring," Meg said. "I used to love them."

"I don't think I've ever seen you eat Cheetos or onion rings," Dad said. "You're more the bean sprouts and tofu type."

"Yeah, well, just thinking about Funyuns is making me hungry," Meg told him. "What about you, Emmy? Are you hungry?"

"I don't care," I said.

"*I'm* getting hungry," Dad said.

"Let's eat McDonald's or Wendy's or something like that," Meg said.

"I love what pregnancy has done to your palate," Dad said. He pulled into a drive-thru to get us some lunch. Meg said she didn't want us to eat in the car because she was worried about all the crumbs, but Dad said if we stopped to eat, we might be late. I knew it was really because Dad hates taking too many breaks when he's driving. He likes to get where he's going as quickly as possible. The woman in the drive-thru window handed Dad the bags of food, and Dad passed my burger and soda over his shoulder to the backseat. I had my pills in my backpack, and I took them out and swallowed them down with my soda. I just wanted the ride to be over. I felt so messed up because I didn't really want to get to camp, but I didn't want to be in the car anymore, either.

A little while later, Dad made a left turn by a wooden sign that had a drawing of a teepee carved into it and big block letters that said CAMP FIREBIRD. When we got there, the bus was already there. Someone bounded over to us. She was wearing a T-shirt that said *Be Positive* on it, and she had a round button pinned to her shirt with a picture of a little girl. "Hey, I'm Robin!" she said. She seemed so excited to be Robin. I wanted to say, *Congratulations!*

"Hi, Robin, I'm Bryan Price," Dad said. "We spoke on the phone. This is my wife, Meg, and this is Emerson. She likes to be called Emmy."

"Welcome to Camp Positive, Emmy!" Robin practically shouted. She moved forward to give me a hug. That's one thing I really hate, strangers hugging you like they know you.

When Robin let go, I looked around. We were standing on a big lawn. I didn't see anyone else there with their parents. Kids were mostly hanging out in little groups. Past the lawn and up a hill, there were a few small buildings. All I ever knew about camp was what I saw on *The Parent Trap*, which was a movie Nicole's mom had rented for us. These girls go to camp and do all these outdoor activities and play tricks on each other. Then they find out that they're each other's long-lost sister. But of course Camp Positive wasn't a normal camp. Even without the long-lost-sister part, it wouldn't be anything like the camp in *The Parent Trap*. Dad asked Robin about my suitcase, and she called someone over to carry it up to the bunk for me. "We're going to get started in a few minutes," Robin said. "So I'll let you say your good-byes." She walked away. I knew it wouldn't do any good if I begged Dad and Meg not to make me stay. They each stepped forward to hug me. I stiffened my body and didn't hug back, so it was like they were hugging a statue.

A few minutes after Dad and Meg left, Robin put two fingers to her mouth and whistled incredibly loudly. Everyone gathered around her in a big circle. Well, mostly everyone—some other kids were hanging out nearby, but they didn't join us. Maybe they already knew everything Robin was going to say. All in all, there were about fifty kids in the circle, which wasn't as many as I expected. In *The Parent Trap*, it seemed like there were hundreds of kids.

"Welcome, Camp Positive campers!" Robin called out. The kids around me started clapping and cheering. I didn't join in. "We have some newbies here this year," Robin continued. "I want to wish them an extra-special welcome." The whole circle shouted, "Welcome!" and there was more clapping and cheering. It seemed to go on an awfully long time.

When the noise finally died down, Robin said she was going to go over a few things for the new campers, as well as for the returning campers who may have forgotten. She explained that she had started Camp Positive ten years before. Her niece had had AIDS. Her name was Brooke, and she'd had a really hard time fitting in with other people. The kids in her school didn't really understand what it was like for her, and some of them were afraid of her. She spent a lot of time sick and alone. A couple of years after Brooke died, Robin decided she wanted to start a camp so she could give girls like her niece a safe place to go. Robin tapped the button pinned to her shirt. I knew it had to be a photo of her niece. "Things have changed since Brooke died," Robin said. "Medications keep improving, as you know, and that is wonderful. But girls with HIV can still feel different and alone, so this is still your safe place. We're all in this together. You can fit in, have fun, and most of all, have the most POSITIVE experience!"

People started cheering again. I groaned a little bit. I didn't think anyone could hear me with all the shouting going on, but someone next to me whispered, "Isn't it all so dumb?"

I turned and saw a girl leaning toward me. She was thin, black, and very pretty. I wondered if her parents had also forced her to come to Camp Positive. "What?" I asked.

"Don't get me wrong," she said, her voice still low. "Robin's great and all. But she can be so corny. She loves those stupid plays on words—Camp Positive, Be Positive, HIV-Positive. It's a little much, don't you think?"

"Yeah, I do," I said.

"I'm Whitney," the girl said. "It's my third summer here."

"I'm Emmy," I said. "I'm new."

"I know," Whitney said. She smiled and turned back to listen to Robin, who had started talking again. Robin explained that Camp Positive shared the area with another camp, Camp Firebird—I was sure it was a normal camp for healthy kids—but other than that, we were really separate. We had the same mess hall, lake, and some other facilities, but we had our own bunks and did our own activities. So that explained the kids who hadn't joined the circle when Robin whistled. Robin also said our camp had its own medical staff, including a doctor, Francesca Vance, and several physician's assistants and nurses—I wondered if the normal kids' camp had its own medical staff. She talked about medication schedules and how we shouldn't worry because the doctor already had all our medication and Camp Positive would accommodate everyone's individual needs, and we could go to the infirmary at any time because someone would always be there. I was sure the kids at Firebird didn't get a speech like that. She also said that no one would make us do any activities that we didn't want to, which was why we had filled out the interest questionnaires. She expected us to participate and give everything a try at least once. *Fat chance,* I thought.

Then Robin went on to tell us about the rules—how we all had to respect each other, and what time we were expected to be in our bunks at night, and how we weren't allowed to wander off without telling anyone. We also weren't allowed to use cell phones. If we needed to call home for any reason, Robin said we should find her and she would let us call from our office. I wondered if she would ever let me call Lisa, even though that wasn't technically calling home.

Robin asked if there were any questions, but nobody said anything, and I certainly wasn't going to ask about Lisa right there in front of everyone else. "Whew, I'm glad that's out of the way," she said, as though all of those rules had exhausted her. "Now I'd like to introduce some very important people." She introduced the medical staff, and then she called out the names of the counselors. They all lined up next to Robin and took turns saying a little bit about themselves. A couple of them said they had been campers at Camp Positive and loved it so much they came back. I guess that meant they were infected too, but nobody said that out loud.

When the introductions were over, the campers were sorted into bunks. The counselors took turns calling out names, and kids would run from the circle to stand next to their counselor. I stood there and waited. Finally one of the counselors—her name was Amanda—called out my name: "Emerson Price!"

I started walking toward her. "She likes to be called Emmy," I heard Robin tell Amanda. Then Robin called out, "Emmy Price!" I was halfway to Amanda already, so I don't know why my name had to be called twice.

Amanda called out a couple of other names. I wasn't really listening until she said, "Whitney Richter!"

Whitney ran over to our group. Her legs were really thin. The way she moved reminded me of that animal that sort of leaps when it runs—was it a gazelle? Whitney stopped next to me. "How cool that we're in the same bunk," she said.

"Okay, Bunk Seven, we're all here," Amanda said. "Let's head inside so we can get settled." Amanda started walking up the lawn toward the buildings. The other girls followed her, and I followed too. It's not like I had any other choice.

Chapter 13

There were six campers in our bunk. Besides Whitney and me, we had Marley, Natalie, Kyla, and Alexis. The beds were set up in pairs—three pairs of two. Each pair of beds had a set of shelves between them. Also, we each had a drawer under our beds. Amanda had a bed off in the corner, sort of away from the rest of us. It was already all made up, and her stuff was unpacked and on shelves. They must have made the counselors come up to Camp Positive a day or two early.

I had the bed next to Natalie. I knew it was my bed because my suitcase was next to it, and there were a couple of envelopes with my name on them on top of the pillows. I recognized Dad's handwriting on one of them. The other envelope was a little bigger, like there was something in it besides just a card. Meg's handwriting was on the front of it. I decided I didn't care about whatever was inside of it.

Amanda said we should all take some time to unpack and settle in. She was going to be in her little corner, and call us over, one at a time, so she could get to know us and fill out some paper-work. I knew Dad had sent a bunch of forms into camp, and he had Dr. Green's office fax my medical stuff, so I wondered what other paperwork there could possibly be. Amanda called Marley first, and I turned toward my suitcase to start unpacking.

I thought about the last time I had unpacked a big suitcase—when I had moved out of Mom's house and into my room at Dad's house. Of course that last time I'd had more than one suitcase, along with boxes and some of the furniture from my old room. It was weird to think of "the last time" and have it be a time *after* Mom died. I didn't like doing so many things without her, but the time without her was just getting longer and longer. I was doing things now that she didn't even know about. I took everything out of the suitcase and started filling up my half of the shelves. There wasn't any real order to how I was unpacking, which was kind of the opposite of nesting, and that made me really glad. I made it look extra haphazard. I liked that word, "haphazard," because it sounded disorganized and messy. Whoever made it up made a word that sounds exactly right. The only things I was careful about were the envelope of pictures and Mom's books. I put them in the drawer under my bed.

"You could put your books on the shelf if you want," Natalie said. "I don't have that much stuff, so there's plenty of room."

I didn't really want Mom's books out in the open. "That's okay," I said.

A couple of minutes later, Amanda called my name. I stuffed the envelopes from Dad and Meg into the corner of one of the shelves. I would've put them in the drawer under the bed, but I didn't want anything from Dad and Meg to be too close to Mom's books. Then I walked over to Amanda's bed. She patted it to let me know that I should sit down. I sat on the edge of the bed and pulled at a strand of my hair. In the last couple of weeks, my hair had grown a little bit and it didn't look as bad. If I put on a headband, or clipped it on either side, it almost looked normal. But it still felt short and strange to me, like it wasn't really mine.

"Hey, Emmy," Amanda said. "You can relax."

"I'm okay," I said.

"Good," she said. "Well, first of all, I just wanted to say welcome—welcome to camp, and welcome to our bunk."

"Thanks," I said.

"Have you ever been to camp before?"

"No," I said.

"Well," Amanda said, "I know I'm technically the counselor here, but it's not like I'm a dictator or anything . . . not like teachers in school sometimes think they are. I'm more like a friend who just happens to be a little older, and happens to turn the lights in the bunk out at the same time every night. So you should feel free to come to me to talk about anything."

"Okay," I said.

"Robin gave me your file and medication schedule. The doctor and her staff also have everything they need where that's concerned, and they'll make sure you get it on time every day. Is there anything else you think I should know? Any side effects from the pills?"

I didn't like the idea that there was a file about me being passed around. "Not really," I said.

"That's good," Amanda said. "Do you get homesick?"

I'd been homesick ever since I moved to Dad's house, but I knew that wasn't what Amanda meant. "I don't know," I said. "I've never been to camp before." I wondered if it would even be possible to get homesick for Dad's house. I mean, Mom's house still felt more like *home* to me.

"I think you'll be okay here," she said. "This is a really good camp to have as your first. When I was your age, I went to another sleepaway camp and they didn't even have bathrooms in the bunk. Can you imagine that? You had to walk around the building through a little wooded area, even if it was the middle of the night. It was completely awful."

I wondered what kind of camp it was—if it was also a camp for kids infected with AIDS, or if it was for normal, healthy kids. Amanda wasn't one of the counselors who had been a camper at Camp Positive, so it was possible she wasn't even infected. I wondered if she had it, or if someone else in her family did.

"Any questions?" Amanda asked.

I couldn't think of anything to ask about camp, and I wasn't going to ask her anything about her family. It wasn't any of my business. Besides, I didn't plan on getting to know anyone that well anyway. "No," I said.

"Okay," she said. "If you think of anything, you know where to find me."

I stood up from Amanda's bed, and she called Kyla over. Later on, our empty suitcases were taken away so they could be stored somewhere. Amanda took us on a little tour of the camp, so we could see where things like the art cabin, the infirmary, and the lake were. Then we went to the mess hall for dinner. I almost wished Meg were there, just so she would have to go to a place called a mess hall, but when we got inside it wasn't any messier than a regular cafeteria. The only real difference was that the tables were made of wood, kind of like picnic benches, instead of the plastic ones we had at school.

Amanda led us to the food, and then pointed out where we'd be eating. We had eight tables on the far side of the room. The Firebird kids were in the mess hall too, but everyone from Camp Positive sat together. It seemed kind of strange, like we were quarantined or something. I wondered why we didn't just have our own camp.

I sat down on a bench in between Whitney and Natalie. Whitney took the bottle of ketchup from the center of the table and squirted a swirly red line onto her hot dog. Then she held out the bottle to me. "Want some?"

"Thanks," I said. I squirted some ketchup onto my plate so I could dip my hot dog into it. That's how I always ate hot dogs—I dipped each bite. I never put the ketchup on top of the hot dog in a line like Whitney did. To me, that looked too much like a vein, and then I always thought of blood and ended up not wanting to eat it.

I dipped the tip of my hot dog into the ketchup and took a bite. It tasted like a normal hot dog and not some gross healthy imitation. A woman came up to our table. I recognized her from orientation that afternoon. She was one of the physician's assistants who Robin had introduced. "Hi, girls," she said. "Sorry to interrupt. I'm Joanna Wallace—one of the PAs here. I have evening meds for Alexis, Emerson, and Kyla." I hated that she said "meds" instead of "medication," like we were all so familiar with it that we could use an abbreviation instead of the whole word. Regular people never said "meds." The only people I'd ever heard use that word were sick people or people who worked with sick people.

Joanna Wallace gave me my pills and I held them in my hand. My palm was kind of sweaty and they stuck to my skin. I'd never taken my pills out in the open like that, in the middle of a packed cafeteria. I glanced around. Kyla had swallowed her pills so quickly that she was already done, and Alexis's head was tipped back as she took hers. I was so used to feeling different, but of course no one at Camp Positive would think having to taking pills was a big deal. We might not all be on the same exact schedule, and we might have different dosages, but chances were that everyone had to deal with taking pills at some point during the day—probably more than once. I swallowed my pills and finished my hot dog.

A bunch of conversations were happening around me, just like in a regular cafeteria. Whitney was talking to a girl sitting across the table. I could tell the other girl had also been to Camp Positive before by the way she and Whitney were talking, like they already knew things about each other. "How's your sister?" the girl asked Whitney.

"She's good," Whitney said. She picked up a carrot stick off her plate and took a bite.

"What's her name again?" the girl asked.

Whitney chewed and swallowed. "Rebecca," she said. "But I don't see her as much as I used to. They moved kind of far away."

"God, I wish my sister would move far away," the girl said. "She's driving the rest of us crazy."

It was weird to hear people talking about their families like that. For some reason, I thought conversations at Camp Positive would sound different. Whitney poked me in the side and asked me where I was from. "Connecticut," I said.

I hoped she wouldn't ask me anything about my family. She picked up the last carrot stick on her plate and took a bite. "Oh gross," she said. "This carrot's bad. I love carrots, but I hate how some of them just don't taste right. You can never tell just by looking at them when they're going to be rotten, you know?"

I shrugged. "I'm not really into carrots," I said.

"Well, trust me," she said. "Sometimes they have this weird bitter taste and it's disgusting . . . oh my God, you know what I just thought? What if the only carrot you ever tasted was one of the bad ones? You'd never know what they're really supposed to taste like!"

"I've tasted more than one carrot," I said. "I just don't like them."

Whitney shrugged. "Oh well, it was just a theory," she said. "Come on. I'll show you where we have to drop our trays." She led me over to a cart at the back of the room that had shelves for all the dirty trays, and I slid my tray onto an empty space. "At Firebird, every bunk has dish duty for a week, which means they have to wash all these trays," Whitney explained. "But we don't ever have to do it. It's mainly because Robin hates doing dishes, and she didn't want us to ever have to be on dish duty. So that's lucky, right?"

"Yeah," I said. What a little thing to be lucky about.

Later that night we were back in the bunk and Amanda turned out the lights. I wasn't used to sleeping in a room with six other people and I could hear all of them shifting in their beds, trying to get comfortable. I rolled over onto my stomach and pressed the side of my head into my pillow. I covered my other ear with part of my blanket, but I could still hear things. I could hear Natalie in the next bed, breathing in and out, in and out. Outside there were weird little noises. I felt like we were out in the middle of nowhere. I hadn't even told anyone where I was going. If Dad and Meg were in some sort of accident and had amnesia, no one would know where to find me. I was still most worried about Mom being able to find me.

I wondered if it was possible to send out a kind of signal to Mom, like those commercials for that thing you can put in your car. It sends out some sort of invisible waves, and then you can find your car if it's stolen. I squeezed my eyes shut and concentrated. The skin around my eyes started to hurt. Once, when I was younger, Mom and I went away with Nicole and her family over Christmas. Nicole was scared that Santa wouldn't know where to find her, and she wouldn't get any presents.

But Mrs. Lister said Santa had the ability to just know where she was. He would always be able to find her.

Across the room I could hear someone crying. I relaxed the muscles around my eyes, but I didn't open them. If I were crying, I wouldn't want anyone to look at me. I heard footsteps, and then Amanda's voice, very soft, saying, "It's all right, it's all right." I shifted in bed and opened my eyes ever so slightly. I could see Amanda sitting on Marley's bed, her arms wrapped around Marley. Marley was leaning into her, letting Amanda hold her, even though they barely knew each other. I wondered if Marley was just homesick, or if it had something to do with having AIDS. Whatever it was, I knew I would never let Amanda or anyone else at Camp Positive hold me like that. I couldn't imagine it would ever make me feel any better.

Chapter 14

I didn't remember falling asleep, but I must have, because I woke up and I couldn't remember where I was. Everything was a little bit fuzzy since I was still so close to dreaming, and nothing felt the way it was supposed to. The mattress wasn't soft enough to be mine. This wasn't my bed. My heart started to beat harder and faster, and the thumping in my chest woke me up all the way. That's when I noticed Natalie in the bed across from me. I made myself breathe deeper so my heart would stop racing. Natalie's arms were crossed on top of her pillow, and her head was rested in the middle. She was sleeping so neatly and so soundly that she looked like a doll.

I strained to hear if anyone else was awake, but I didn't hear anyone moving around. I turned over in bed, and it sounded louder than usual, like just the crumpling of sheets was loud enough to break something.

No one else woke up until an alarm that sounded like a whistle went off. I wondered if Robin had taped herself whistling so she could play it in all the bunks and wake everyone up. Amanda got out of bed and announced that we had thirty-five minutes to get ready and head out for breakfast. I watched Natalie get up and grab her towel off the shelf so she could take a shower. I decided there was no point in rushing to take a shower right then. I would go with everyone to the mess hall since I needed to eat to take my pills. But after that, I didn't want to do whatever activity Robin had scheduled, so I would just go back to the bunk and shower then. I planned to stay in the bunk all day, every day, for the whole six weeks, just like I used to hang out in my room all the time at Dad's house. I'd probably finish reading all of Mom's books.

A little while later, we headed over to the mess hall. Even though we had only been at Camp Positive for less than a day, it seemed like kids were already making friends and forming groups, just like at school. Everyone seemed to know who to sit with. There were the kids who knew each other from the summer before. Alexis's sister Claudia was actually the counselor in Bunk Five, so Alexis went to eat with her. Marley and Natalie were new like I was, but I could tell they were going to be best friends. The way they talked and giggled and touched each other's shoulders reminded me of how Nicole and I used to be.

As far as I could tell, I was the only one who had actually been forced to go to Camp Positive. Everyone else seemed happy to be there. I didn't understand it. We were all infected with AIDS, and most of us probably knew at least one person who had died of it. But people were talking and laughing like everything was completely fine. I sat down next to Marley on the end of one of the benches. You couldn't even tell that she'd been crying the night before.

Robin stood up at the next table. "Good morning, Camp Positive campers!" she called out. "I hope you had a good first night of camp and rested up, because this morning is our annual scavenger hunt!"

In *The Parent Trap*, the camp director always yelled into a bullhorn, but Robin didn't even need one. Her voice was loud enough on its own. She went on about the scavenger hunt, but I stopped listening to the actual words, so it all just sounded like background noise, almost like she was speaking another language that I couldn't understand. After Robin finished, Joanna Wallace came over to our table with the morning pills. I had just finished swallowing them when Whitney tapped me on the shoulder. "Hey," she said, "I didn't really get to say hi to you this morning."

"That's okay," I said.

"I just hate mornings," she said. She rubbed her eyes for effect. When she moved her hand back, there was an eyelash stuck to her cheek. It's weird how eyelashes do that instead of just falling off. It's like there's some sort of static electricity in eyelashes that makes them stick to your face, until you pluck them off and make a wish and blow. "I don't see why we have to get up so early here," Whitney continued. "It's not like we have to be at school or anything. But Robin's into the whole early-bird thing."

I wasn't sure what she meant, so I just shrugged.

"Anyway," she said, "I know this scavenger hunt sounds like it's a cheesy bonding thing, but it's actually totally fun. At least it was last year, and our bunk didn't even win. Maybe we'll win this year, though. We have a pretty good bunk."

I realized as she was talking that each bunk must be its own team. Clearly Whitney thought I already knew that. It was probably one of the things that Robin explained while I wasn't paying attention. "Maybe," I said. I didn't tell her that I wasn't planning on being part of any of it, so I didn't really care if the bunk won or lost.

"Don't worry about being new and not knowing the campground that well," Whitney said. "It's not that kind of scavenger hunt. And besides, Kyla, Alexis, and I were all here before, so we'll know where to find things."

Whitney was probably kind of person who volunteered to show the new kids in school around. I could tell she would be good at that kind of job. She seemed to know everything and like everyone. She started talking to Marley and Natalie about the scavenger hunt, and I got up to drop off my tray. I walked over to Amanda to tell her I was just going to head back to the bunk to rest.

"Do you feel okay?" Amanda asked.

"Yeah," I said. "I'm just tired."

"Let me go get Dr. Vance," Amanda said. "I'm sure she'll want you to rest in the infirmary, just to be safe."

"You don't need to get Dr. Vance," I said.

"It's camp policy," Amanda said. "It's not a big deal—a bunch of campers take naps in the infirmary every day, so you wouldn't be the only one."

Naptime for the sick kids, I thought. I bet Camp Firebird didn't have a naptime. "It's not that I feel sick," I said. "I just don't really want to do the scavenger hunt."

"Oh come on, Emmy," Amanda said. "We all promised Robin we'd participate in the activities here."

I hadn't promised Robin anything. Robin had said the thing about participating in her opening speech, but it's not like I agreed to it. Maybe it had been on one of the forms that Dad filled out, but that shouldn't count.

I could tell by the way Amanda was looking at me that she really expected me to be a joiner and go on the scavenger hunt with them. I wanted to tell her I wasn't that kind of girl—I wasn't like her, or Whitney, or Robin, or anyone else at Camp

Positive. I couldn't just pretend everything was fine and be happy. But I wasn't sure how to say it. If Dad was the one telling me I should give it a try, I probably would've shouted at him about not wanting to go on his stupid scavenger hunt. Why was it easier to say no to Dad than to a stranger? It didn't make any sense. It should be the other way around. After all, it's not like Amanda could do anything to punish me. It's not like I would even ever have to see her again after the summer.

But instead I just said something stupid. "I didn't even shower. I planned on going back to the bunk to shower after breakfast."

"Don't worry about it, Emmy," Amanda said. "You'll have plenty of time to take a shower afterward. Besides, you look great. This'll be fun."

So that's how I ended up heading outside with the rest of the crowd. Robin was on the lawn, right where we'd had orientation the day before. But instead of a big circle, we stood in little clusters with our bunkmates. Alexis was practically jumping up and down. "You guys, we have to beat Claude's bunk. Her bunk won last year, and she went on and on about it."

Robin gave us our instructions. She said each of the counselors had a digital camera, which we would need for the scavenger hunt. Then she went around handing each of the groups a different colored package. Our package was blue. Inside were the rest of the supplies we would need, along with our first clue. As soon as every group had an envelope, Robin whistled again. I was going to hate listening to that whistle for the next six weeks. Amanda ripped open our package—there was a pad of paper and pencils. She read out loud from a piece of blue paper: "Cross out six letters to find the location of your next clue."

"What are the six letters?" Whitney asked.

"There's just a jumble of letters after that," Amanda said. "I guess we have to figure out what letters to cross out in order to make a word. Sorry guys, I'm not that good at word puzzles."

Everyone bent over the piece of paper with the letters on it. "It doesn't make any sense," Natalie said. "Even if we cross out six of the letters, I don't see how it would make any words. There are just too many letters jumbled up."

"Come on you guys," Alexis said. "We can do this."

Amanda gave us each a piece of paper and a pencil so we could copy the letters and try to figure out what we were supposed to cross out. We sat in a little circle on the ground. I rolled the pencil between my palms and stared down at the letters: *ASIRXTLE CTATBERISN*. I wasn't actually trying to solve it. It seemed like another language, like when Robin had made her announcement at breakfast and everything blurred together and didn't sound like anything recognizable.

Amanda's voice came from behind me. "Got any ideas, Emmy?" she asked.

"Not really," I said.

"I've got it," Whitney said all of a sudden. "It's the art cabin."

"It can't be," Kyla said. "Even if you cross out six letters, there are still too many left over to spell that out."

"No, that's the trick," Whitney said. "You don't cross out six letters. You cross out the words 'six letters.' See?" She held up her piece of paper with *S-I-X-L-E-T-T-E-R-S* crossed out. In between the cross-outs were the leftover letters, and Whitney was right. They spelled "ART CABIN."

"All right!" Alexis said. She jumped up like a cheerleader. "Whitney, you're a genius!"

"No, I'm not," Whitney said, but I could tell she was proud to have figured it out.

"Let's get going then," Amanda said.

"But what if the other bunks follow us?" Natalie asked.

"Everyone has a different word jumble so we'll end up in different places," Amanda said. "Just don't tell them the secret to figuring it out. Come on."

We raced toward the art cabin. There was a blue envelope pinned to the front door. Alexis got to it first and tore it open. "Okay, guys," she said. "This is what the camera is for. We're supposed to take pictures of seven things in this order: a squirrel, something purple, a cone from an evergreen tree, something flying, something with lace, a tree that's too big to fit your arms around, and a teepee."

"Well there are tons of squirrels around here," Kyla said. "That can't be too hard to find."

"It's always harder when you're looking for it," Amanda said.

"Hey look, there's a bird," Marley said. "That can be our something flying. Quick, take a picture."

"No," Alexis said. "We're supposed to take the pictures in order, and that's the fourth thing." The whole thing seemed so dumb to me, but of course I didn't say anything.

Amanda suggested that we walk behind the bunks, toward the woods. She said the squirrels would probably be back there, and maybe we'd spot some purple flowers along the way, so we'd know where to go back to after we got our squirrel photo. "Do you want to be the photographer, Emmy?" she asked, holding the camera out to me.

"It's all right," I said. "Someone else can do it." Amanda handed the camera to Whitney.

Alexis was at the head of the pack, leading us around the back of the art cabin and past the bunks, toward the woods. "I think I see something moving," she said. Whitney jogged a little to catch up. I watched the way the dust rose up as she ran.

Her foot landed in one spot, and there was a little cloud of dust. Before the dust had settled back down, there was another little cloud at her next step. If I had the camera, I would've liked to take a picture of that—of the way the little particles of dirt were still moving, even after she had gone on.

"There's one!" Kyla said. Whitney stopped running. I heard the little click the camera made when she pushed the button down.

"I hope you got it," Kyla said. "He ran away as soon as you took the picture."

Whitney looked at the little screen on the back of the camera. "Don't worry," she said. "I got it."

Marley leaned over Whitney's shoulder to check the screen herself, as if Whitney might've been wrong. "Wow, he's just barely in the corner of the picture," she said. "We almost missed him."

"That's awesome, Whitney," Amanda said. "You're two for two."

They were all grinning about the squirrel, as if they'd taken a picture of something truly amazing—like a spaceship or a unicorn. Alexis reminded everyone that we had to find something purple next. We hadn't seen any purple flowers on our way to the woods, but Kyla suddenly squealed. "Oh my God, you guys, I just thought of something. My toes are purple! I mean, my toenails are—I painted them a couple of days ago. The color is even called Purple Rain." She kicked off one of her sneakers and wiggled her toes. Whitney stood over her with the camera.

The next few things weren't that hard to find. Marley plucked a pinecone from a branch that had fallen off a tree, so we got that picture. Then there was a sparrow walking along the path, and Alexis ran up behind it. Whitney was waiting with the camera to take a picture when it got scared and started to fly away. For something with lace, Amanda pointed out a wildflower that she said was called Queen Anne's Lace, so we took a picture of that. After that, we walked around hugging trees, trying to find one with a trunk that was too big to fit our arms around. I wondered how old the trees were. I had once heard if you cut down a tree, you could tell how old it was by how many rings there were. Each ring was supposed to count for a year.

"I'm the shortest so I should probably hug all the trees," Marley said.

"What do you mean?" Alexis asked.

"I have the shortest arms," Marley told her. "Your height is the length of your arms from tip to tip."

I wrapped my arms around a tree and thought about something Uncle Rob had said a couple of years before. He and Aunt Laura were visiting Mom and me. Rob was sitting at the kitchen table reading the paper. When he finished he stood up and threw it away in the garbage under the sink. I told him that was all wrong. There was a recycling program in Highlands, and Mom had bought special garbage cans for soda bottles and newspapers. "It goes over there," I told him, pointing to the blue basket in the corner by the side of the fridge. "Or else they'll have to kill more trees, just so you can read your papers."

Uncle Rob pulled the newspaper back out of the trash and put it in the right place. He walked over to the counter where I was sitting. I liked to hoist myself up on the island between the table and the sink. He tapped my knees with his fingers. "So you're a tree hugger now," he said. "You're a better man than I am."

I didn't know what he was talking about, but there I was at Camp Positive, actually hugging a tree. I could clasp my hands together on the other side, so it wasn't the right tree for the scavenger hunt, but I didn't let go right away.

"Hey, I got one!" Marley called out.

Whitney took the picture, and then we only had the teepee left. "I've been at Camp Positive for two summers," Alexis said. "I can't remember ever seeing a teepee here."

"Well there's gotta be one somewhere if it's on the list," Kyla said.

"Maybe we're supposed to make one and then take a picture," Natalie said.

"I don't know," Whitney said.

"Why not?" Natalie asked. "It's not like it's in the rules that we can't make it, right? Are there supplies in the art cabin that we could use?"

"But this is the last thing on the list," Alexis said. "I think we're supposed to find an actual teepee—that's where the next clue will be."

I leaned back against the tree and waited for them to decide what to do. It was only the second day, and time was moving so slowly. I remembered driving into camp with Dad and Meg the day before. It seemed like it had been at least a week ago, maybe even longer. I thought of the sign that said CAMP FIREBIRD at the entrance, with the little drawing of a teepee carved into it. I heard the words coming out of my mouth before I realized what I was doing. "Hey, I know where to find one."

We ran down the dirt road to the camp entrance, and sure enough, there was a blue envelope tacked to the CAMP FIREBIRD sign. "Way to go, Emmy!" Amanda cried. She put her arm around my shoulder and squeezed. Whitney took a picture of the teepee while Kyla read the next clue. "Oh no, Amanda," she said. "It's another kind of logic puzzle."

"Read it out loud," Amanda said.

"Okay, here goes: There's a man who leaves home. He heads right, and then makes a left turn and goes exactly the same distance, makes another left turn and goes exactly the same distance again, and makes another left turn and runs the exact same distance until he reaches home again."

"So what's the point of that?" Marley asked.

"I guess that's what we have to figure out," Amanda said.

Alexis picked up a stick and started on tracing the ground—right, left, left, left. "It's a square," she said. "I don't get it." She tossed the stick back onto the ground. "Oh, this is so annoying. I bet Claudia's bunk already finished."

"Don't give up so easily," Amanda said.

Natalie bent down by the square Alexis had made. She stared at it like she was studying really hard. It was like when Nicole would stare at her flashcards and try to memorize how the words looked. Natalie moved over a little so she was sitting at one of the points of the square. "Of course," she said. "Guys, look at it this way and it's really obvious. It's like a diamond."

Marley stood behind her. "I still don't get it," she said.

"It's a baseball diamond—you know. It's not a house. It's *home*. He was playing baseball, and he was running home, like a home run."

"Oh my God, that's it!" Alexis said. "Come on, let's go! Hurry!"

We ran to the baseball diamond. Robin was there with Dr. Vance and Joanna Wallace and a few other people who I recognized from orientation. "Congratulations, Bunk Seven!" they called out. They had set up a pizza party for lunch, with boxes of pizza on the benches by the side of the field. Alexis started high-fiving everyone, and Robin told us to dig in and enjoy. The other bunks trickled in one by one and got to eat pizza too. I wasn't sure what the point of winning was if we all got the same thing in the end. Then Robin made a speech about teamwork and how everyone was a winner, and we were all "positively great." She walked around and gave out different-colored rib-

bons. Our bunk got the blue ones. I watched Alexis march over
to Claudia and dangle it in front of her. Claudia swatted at it.

I swallowed hard. My mouth felt really dry. There was a
cooler right by home plate, so I walked over to get a bottle of
water. I twisted off the cap and took a big gulp. Amanda came
over and grabbed a soda from the cooler. "Great job on the teepee," she said. "I never would have thought of that. We might
not have won if you had stayed in the bunk, you know."

"I guess," I said.

"So, what did you think?" she asked. "It wasn't so bad, was it?"

It really hadn't been so bad, but I couldn't admit that to
Amanda since I hadn't wanted to go in the first place. I didn't
think I was supposed to have fun. I started to shrug, but Amanda
reached out to squeeze my shoulder again, so I don't think she
even noticed.

Chapter 15

It turned out that camp was kind of like school. Each day was broken up into different time periods. The difference was that at school those periods were for classes, and at camp they were for activities—things like softball and yoga and pottery and capture the flag. Some activities were "bunk activities," which meant you were assigned to do something with everyone else in your bunk. Sometimes we had "interest-based activities," which meant kids from different bunks were grouped together based on that questionnaire about our interests—the one Dad had filled out for me. And then there were the "campwide activities," which meant everyone at Camp Positive participated in them all at once. At the end of the day we sang songs that everyone seemed to know the words to. Robin was really into having a campfire after dinner and roasting marshmallows, so we did that a lot too.

It was good to not have Dad or Meg around, watching everything I did, and I was so busy at camp that I barely had time to think about them. But the most important thing was that Mom didn't feel as far away as she did when I was in Highlands. At home, it was like everything I did reminded me she wasn't there. At camp, it was normal not to have your parents around. It didn't feel like Mom was missing.

We had been at camp about a week when Robin made an announcement at breakfast that it was time for an activity called the Write Words. At first I thought she meant the *Right* Words, but she passed out sheets of paper to all of us, and it was written across the top the other way. I knew it had to be another one of her plays on words. She went on about how this was a camp-wide activity, so we all had to do it. We would be broken up into smaller groups, and each group would be led by a member of the medical staff, along with a couple of the counselors. She said we should write out any questions we had about AIDS on the paper she had handed out.

"There are no wrong questions, and no stupid questions," Robin said. "Everything you *write* is *right*, and I want you to feel free to ask anything and everything."

I looked down at the paper Robin had passed out. I wanted to write, *Why us?* But I knew that wasn't the kind of question Robin had in mind.

Robin whistled a few minutes later, which was our signal to go outside. I was assigned to Joanna Wallace's group. We sat in a circle on the grass behind the mess hall. Kyla and Marley were in my group, along with a few campers from other bunks, Alexis's sister Claudia, and another counselor named Vanessa. Everyone folded up their papers and passed them to Joanna. I folded up mine too, even though I hadn't written anything down. I passed it up like everyone else did.

Joanna took a couple of minutes to read over the questions. I watched her flip through the pages. She didn't say anything about one of the sheets being blank. When she was done, she said she was going to start with the questions about "meds." There was that word again. I really didn't want to sit there in a circle and talk about all the pills we had to take. Joanna read the first question out loud, but I wasn't really listening. I glanced up at the sky and remembered that song Nicole had talked about, the one about looking up at the same big sky.

I wondered what Nicole was doing right then. Maybe she was looking at the sky, thinking about Brody Hudson. Or maybe Zach Andrews started liking her back, and she didn't even care about Brody anymore. I wanted to know, but I tried not to care. It wasn't like Nicole would write me a letter about it. She didn't even know where I was, because I didn't tell her. I guess if she wanted to, she could find out. She could call my house and ask Dad or Meg. Meg was so into meddling in things, she would definitely give Nicole my address. I bet she'd even offer to help her write me a letter. Not that Nicole would even want to write to me—she was probably too mad. And if she did, I might not even read it. I might just stick it on the shelf next to the letters from Dad and Meg.

I didn't want to think about anyone in Highlands anymore. I scrunched my eyes up and rubbed them a little. When I looked up, I caught Joanna Wallace looking at me from across the circle. She probably thought that I was thinking hard. I looked away from her, up at the sky again. It looked almost exactly the way it had that day at school. Maybe, just maybe, Nicole was looking up at it and thinking of me.

"Okay," Joanna said loudly, "let's change gears a bit and talk about boys."

A few months before, we'd had these health classes in school, which was the school's version of sex education. Kids giggled for practically the whole time that Ms. Taylor was talking. But everyone in the circle was looking at Joanna seriously.

Joanna talked a little bit about how it was important to understand how you could and couldn't get AIDS—you can't get AIDS from hugging or kissing someone. You could get it from having sex, but there were safe ways to do that, too, when we were old enough. Obviously, I knew all that, but I still wondered sometimes if any of it would ever happen to me. That's why I hated when Nicole started talking about boys. Then Joanna said, "Here's a question: When do you have to tell someone that you're HIV-positive?"

"I think you should be up front about it," Kyla said. "I think you should tell a guy right away, even before you kiss him."

"I don't think so," a girl named Jasmine said. She was one of the campers in Claudia's bunk. "I think if you're just getting to know a guy, you don't have to say anything. It's not like you can get it from kissing."

"Yeah," Kyla said, "but what if you end up telling him later and he gets mad because you lied?"

"It's not lying if you don't say anything," Jasmine said. "Besides, what if you just kiss him, and then you never do anything again? It wouldn't be a big deal. But if you told him, he might hate you for it, and then blab it to the whole school. Right now, no one in my school really knows I have AIDS."

"It could get out anyway," Kyla said. "I wouldn't want someone else to tell a guy that I was infected, so I would tell him myself before that happened."

"God, this sucks," Jasmine said. "I mean, why can't we just have fun if we're not hurting anyone? Why can't we be like everyone else? If you tell a boy you have HIV just because you think he might kiss you, he might tell everyone else and ruin your whole life. And then you didn't get kissed anyway." Jasmine's voice cracked like she was starting to cry. Marley was sitting next to her, and she patted Jasmine's knee.

"I'm not public at school either," another girl said. "I think about it all the time. Not just about boys, but about my friends. I just want to be able to tell them who I am. It makes me so tired sometimes, to just remember to keep pretending. And sometimes I totally convince myself that I'm just like everyone else, and I forget to do things like take my pills and stuff. Then it just comes crashing back."

I wondered if it was better to pretend everything was normal and have everyone like you, or if it was better to have everyone know so you didn't have to pretend. Sometimes I felt like Nicole was pretending to like me, just because I had HIV and she felt bad for me. Or maybe she wasn't pretending. She didn't seem to get tired of pretending, and I could remember lots of times when we actually had fun together, so maybe it was really real. My legs were started to cramp from sitting cross-legged for so long, so I shifted positions and drew my legs up to my chest. "Yes, Emmy?" Joanna asked.

"Oh no," I said. "I didn't say anything."

"Well, is there anything you want to say? How do you feel about all of this?"

I shrugged. "I agree that it sucks," I told her.

Joanna nodded, seriously, like I had said something very wise. "So when do you think you need to tell someone you have HIV?"

"I don't know," I said. "Everyone at my school has just always known, so I've never really had to deal with telling anyone."

"Do you think it's easier that way, not having to pretend?"

"I guess," I said. "But there's still stuff to pretend about."

"Like what?" Joanna asked.

I shifted positions again, so I was sitting Indian-style. "Like my best friend. She knows that I'm HIV-positive, and she's never acted scared of me, but she doesn't know how it feels. Sometimes she'll start talking about some boy she has a crush on, and it just makes me so mad, but I can't tell her that I'm mad because it's not like she really did anything wrong."

It was weird to be telling everyone how it felt to be me. I was used to keeping it inside. But they nodded like they understood. I wondered what it would be like in a school where no one knew I was infected. If Aaron Bay didn't know about AIDS, maybe he would look at me and think I was pretty. Maybe he would be my first kiss.

Joanna Wallace turned to Vanessa and Claudia. "How have you two dealt with this?"

"Well, most people in my school don't know," Vanessa said. "But I do have a boyfriend, and he knows my status. He and my best friend are actually the only two people who know. I still remember how completely freaked out I was to tell them—I didn't know what would happen. Especially with Nathan, my boyfriend. But he was totally amazing."

"I know this is going to sound like a cliché," Joanna said, "but if someone doesn't accept you just because you're HIV-positive, it probably isn't someone you want to be around anyway. I know it's easy for me to say, and I know it doesn't feel true when you're worried about being alone, but I really do believe that. Besides, if you lose someone because you were honest, then you didn't really have them in the first place."

"I just still want to know why this had to happen to us at all," Jasmine said.

That was my question, I thought.

"One of my teachers once told me he thought this happened to my family because we were meant to set an example for everyone else, and show them how to deal with something terrible and still be brave," Claudia said. "When he said it, I thought it was complete bull. But sometimes I think I really am setting an example. People come to me when bad things happen because they trust me, and it makes me feel important."

"I'd rather be healthy than important," Vanessa said.

Joanna smiled. "I think everyone can agree on that," she said.

A few minutes later I heard Robin's ridiculously loud whistle again, which meant the Write Words was over. I followed my group to the big lawn. We had a breakdown meeting, and all the group leaders reviewed the themes of our individual discussions. By the end I was so tired. I wished I could go lie down. But I knew that if I told Amanda or Robin that I wanted to rest, they would make me see Dr. Vance.

Robin told everyone to gather around in a big circle. "In case you haven't noticed, we do lots of things in circles," Whitney told me.

"I know," I said. "It kind of reminds me of kindergarten."

I looked around the circle. Jasmine was directly across from me. She wasn't crying anymore. I wondered what she was thinking. We all probably had the same questions. It was so different than being with a group of kids at school in Highlands. At home, I was always the only one infected with AIDS. It felt like people were looking at me because I had this terrible disease and everyone knew it. At camp, everyone still knew I was infected, but I didn't stand out as much. We were all going through the exact same thing—having doctors' appointments, and blood tests, and taking pills every day, and not knowing if we would get to grow up, and be married, and have kids. I knew some of the kids in the circle probably had parents who died too. And they must have loved their parents as much as I loved Mom. There was so much sadness, just right there in that circle. If you gathered it up all together, it would be bigger than the entire universe. I tried to imagine that happening—all our feelings coming out from inside us and moving up together, rising above us, as if feelings were something you could actually see. I felt better and worse, all at the same time. I couldn't decide what I felt more of.

Robin led as all in a stretching exercise, telling us to roll our heads from side to side and lift our arms up way over our heads. Then we had to jump up and down and wiggle our arms. "It's the hokey pokey," Whitney said. "You're right—we are in kindergarten."

At lunch Robin announced the afternoon activities and I found out that I was signed up for the nature walk. I couldn't imagine what Dad had written down as my interests to get me assigned to something like that. It's not like we ever went camping or anything. But luckily Whitney was doing the nature walk too. After we finished eating, we followed a counselor named Tamara toward the woods behind the bunks. Tamara seemed older than the other counselors, like around thirty. She told us she had done an internship at the New York Botanical Garden, and ever since then, she really loved nature. We walked back to the woods and Tamara breathed in deeply enough for us all to hear. "Smell that," she said to no one in particular. "It really makes you feel connected to nature."

I turned to Whitney and she rolled her eyes. "Yeah," she whispered, "this is gonna be lame."

Tamara led us up a little hill. There was a wood-chip trail between the trees that wound around and made it seem like we were walking a lot farther away from the campgrounds than we really were. "Is everyone with me?" she called out. But she didn't turn around to check. We all said yes. "I can't wait to show you the clearing up past the elms," Tamara continued. "There's a field of wildflowers and it's just spectacular." A couple of girls jogged up the path to catch up with Tamara, but I hung back with Whitney, going slower and slower. After a few minutes, we couldn't even see the rest of our group. We could just hear their voices through the trees.

"I was so exhausted after the Write Words that I kind of just wanted to take a nap," Whitney said. "But then Robin would have made me go to Dr. Vance's cabin, and I didn't want to do that either."

"I thought the exact same thing," I said.

"You always take a chance when you do things with Tamara," Whitney said. "Sometimes she's cool, but sometimes she can be really boring, and now I'm totally getting my second wind. Do you want to get out of here?"

"Are you serious?" I asked. Whitney surprised me sometimes. The first day we met, I expected her to be the perfect camper. But she definitely had a rebellious streak.

"Yeah," she said.

"Okay," I told her.

We turned back around and started heading down the hill. You could see the lake through the trees. "Let's go there," Whitney said.

"I don't know," I said. "I think some of the Camp Positive people are swimming and they could see us."

"Don't worry. We won't go by the swimming side. We can go on the side where the Firebird campers canoe and stuff."

There was a little shed by the side of the lake where they stored all the canoes at night, and I followed Whitney over to it. We sat sort of behind the shed, so no one from the swimming side of the lake could see us. It was actually very pretty, the way the light hit the water. The center of the lake was the exact same color as the sky. "Isn't this better than a nature walk?" Whitney said.

"Oh yeah," I said. "No competition."

"Tamara told me this thing last summer, about something called Caesar's last breath, and I thought it was really cool," Whitney said. "I thought that's what the nature thing would be about. That's why I picked it."

"What is it?" I asked.

But Whitney didn't answer. She was looking past me and shaking her head. "Uh-oh," she said. "Someone's walking over here."

I turned behind me and saw a man with a clipboard taking long strides toward us and looking very official. He must have been sent to find us. "Hey, do you two happen to be Candace and Donna?"

I opened my mouth to say no. "That's us," Whitney said quickly. Maybe she thought it was better for us to pretend to be somebody else.

"Great," the man said. "I'm Phil—I'm the canoe man. Now I've met all the advanced swimmers. You two are welcome to take one of the canoes without a counselor—in fact, a spot just opened up, so you can take one now if you want. Just make sure you wear life jackets."

Whitney stood up and looked down at me. "Come on, Candace," she said. "Let's do it."

Phil led us over to a red canoe and gave us each a life jacket and an oar. Whitney sat in front and I sat in back. Phil helped us push off into the lake. I'd never been canoeing before, but after a while I got the hang of it, and Whitney and I coordinated our paddling so we didn't end up going in circles. We made sure to stay far away from the swimmers. I dipped my fingers into the water. "You don't think there's anything gross in the lake, do you?" I called to Whitney.

"People swim in it, so I'm sure it's okay," she said.

"Yeah, you're probably right," I said. "Do you think Tamara and all them have noticed we're missing yet?"

"If they did, they'll never find us here," Whitney said. She turned around to face me and balanced her oar on her lap. "Let's just float for a while before we go back."

"Okay," I said. I leaned back a little, which was kind of hard to do in a canoe. The sun was really bright and it lit up everything. It was like the Sheryl Crow song Mom liked—the sun burning away the darkness. I realized that I actually liked camp, which was odd because I didn't expect to like it at all. But there I was in the middle of a lake, so far away from Highlands, and I was having a good time.

"This is the life," Whitney said.

"I know," I said. "Oh hey, what was that thing you started to tell me by the canoe shed, about Shakespeare's last breath?"

"Caesar's last breath," Whitney said. "I don't really remember it completely, but basically Caesar lived a really long time ago, and supposedly the last breath he exhaled before he died was really, really long. Now all the molecules he exhaled are part of the air around us, so every time we inhale, we take in part of Caesar's breath, and we're connected to this really famous guy."

"That's kind of bizarre," I said.

"I think it's cool," Whitney said. "I like that kind of stuff. It doesn't gross me out, or anything. So anyway, that's why I picked the nature walk. I thought Tamara would tell us more stuff like that. You know, she was one of the first counselors at Camp Positive, back when Robin started the camp. She's had HIV for a really long time. I heard that she was once in a magazine about it, and she got to meet a bunch of famous people—you know how famous people love doing things for sick kids."

"I've never met anyone famous," I said.

"Me either. But maybe someday we will. I have a whole list of people I want to meet," she said. She lifted her arms up to stretch and clasped her hands together above her head. I could hear her knuckles crack. "That's why we're at this camp anyhow."

"What do you mean?" I asked.

"The guy who runs Firebird donated part of the camp to us so Robin could start Camp Positive," Whitney said. "He's one of those people who likes doing nice things for sick kids. I think it makes him feel good about himself, or something."

"How come we don't just have our own camp?" I asked.

"It would be too expensive," Whitney said. "Most camps charge the campers a lot of money, but it's practically free to come to Camp Positive because Robin doesn't have to pay for the campground, or the food, or any of that stuff."

"How do you know?"

"Robin had a big fundraiser for Camp Positive last year, and she asked me to come speak at it. Afterward, she told me she got lots of donations for the camp, so we could all keep coming here. It's a good thing, too. I mean, I'd never be able to come here if we had to pay a lot of money."

I didn't know Dad was sending me to a camp that was practically free. No wonder he was so quick to send me away. He didn't even have to pay for it. Not that I thought he was worried about money. It wasn't like we were millionaires or anything, but we always had money to pay for things we needed. I guess we had enough other problems. Then again, Whitney had the other problems too, and she still had to worry about money.

"You know, I'm starting to feel sort of guilty," Whitney said. For a second I thought she was still talking about the money.

"Yeah, me too," I said. I felt guilty about getting to go to camp for free, and then I felt mad about Dad sending me to a free camp.

"People are probably looking for us," Whitney continued. "Maybe we should head back to shore."

So she wasn't talking about the money after all. "I guess," I said.

Whitney shifted in her seat so we could start paddling again, but as she turned, the oar slipped off her lap and into the water. "Oh no!" she said. She bent over, but the oar had started to sink.

"Can you reach it?" I asked.

"I don't think so," she said. "I thought it would float, but maybe it's defective.

"It's all right," I said. "I still have my oar."

"Yeah, but I don't think we can paddle straight with just one oar. Maybe we should swim."

"We'd never make it back," I said.

"Oh come on, Emmy, you gotta be positive!"

"You sound like Robin," I said.

Whitney put her fingers in her mouth and tried to whistle, but she couldn't do it. Her face turned kind of red. She gave up and pulled her fingers out of her mouth. "Emmy Price, you gotta be positive!" she shouted. I started laughing. Whitney was cheering: "You need to be positively positive! You need to be the positivest!"

I was laughing so hard that I couldn't really breathe, and I gulped for some air. "That's not even a word," I said.

"Whatever," Whitney said. She stood up. "I'm going in. It'll be fine. After all, you're Candace and I'm Donna. We're advanced swimmers."

"Right, Donna," I said. "I almost forgot." Whitney jumped in. I heard her shriek when she hit the water.

"Are you okay?" I called.

"Oh yeah," she said. "It's just a little cold. But actually once you get in and start dog-paddling, it gets a little warmer." She bobbed up and down and grinned.

I put my oar down on the bottom of the canoe and jumped in after her. I dog-paddled next to Whitney, but it didn't seem to get any warmer. We started to head toward the shore. It was harder to move because we were wearing life jackets, and we couldn't swim underwater. But we were making progress. I could see Phil by the canoe shed, waving his arms. There were two girls standing next to him. For all I knew, they could be the real Candace and Donna. "Hey, Whitney, let's slow down a little," I said. "I don't want to get there too fast."

Chapter 16

Robin was really mad. Her face was practically purple as she yelled at us—and Whitney told me later that she'd never seen Robin yell at anyone. It made Whitney cry because she felt so bad. She told Robin she was sorry, and that the whole thing was her idea, so Robin shouldn't be mad at me. "I'm furious with *both* of you," Robin said. "What were the two of you thinking, running off like that?"

I wanted to tell her that we didn't run off—we had just walked away, kind of slowly. And we weren't exactly thinking about it when it happened. It was like the time I walked out of school in the middle of the day. It wasn't for any particular reason. But it was too hard to explain. Robin's eyes darted back and forth between Whitney and me. I didn't want to have to look her in the eye, so I looked above her head, and then down at her chin. I mumbled, "Sorry," and Whitney kept crying.

"While you're here at camp, you're like my kids," Robin

said. "I'm like your parent. And you can't just disappear like that. You can't even imagine how worried I was."

Whitney sniffled loudly. I wondered if she was trying to be dramatic so Robin wouldn't be as mad. "I'm so sorry we worried you," she said. "I've never been so sorry in my life. Please believe me."

"I believe you," Robin said.

"Can you forgive us?" Whitney asked.

"Yes," Robin said, "but you're still going to be punished." She told us we were on dish duty in the mess hall for a whole week. "Breakfast *and* lunch," she said. "The only reason I'm not making you do dishes at dinner, too, is because that's when the Firebird campers are on dish duty, and the kitchen is already pretty crowded at that time."

So the next day, instead of leaving the mess hall after breakfast with everyone else from Camp Positive, Whitney and I had to stick around and wait for all the campers to put their trays on the tray cart. Then we pulled the cart into the kitchen and helped the kitchen staff scrape the leftover food into garbage cans, soak the plates in soapy hot water, and scrub off the stuck-on food before the plates were loaded into the industrial-sized dishwasher. They gave us rubber gloves to wear so we wouldn't have to touch the plates, but the gloves had this gross chalkiness on the inside and they made my hands hot and clammy. And of course we had to do it all over again for lunch.

By the middle of the week, Whitney and I had our routine down. I would pull the trays off the cart and scrape off the food, and then Whitney soaked and scrubbed.

"It doesn't make sense that we have to wash the dishes before they're put in the dishwasher," I said. "What's the point of having the dishwasher then?"

Whitney shrugged. "This was probably the worst punishment that Robin could come up with," she said.

"Yeah, you told me she hates doing dishes."

"It's sort of a pathological thing for her," Whitney said. "She was a waitress once, when she needed money for college, but she had to quit and find another job. She gets really grossed out at the idea of other people's food."

I thought the grossest part was how the food that was stuck to the plates got all slimy from soaking in water. I could barely even look at the sink where Whitney was scrubbing the plates. But Whitney didn't seem to mind that much. She was humming one of the camp songs as she cleaned. "Come on," she said. "Sing with me."

"I don't know the words," I told her.

"I bet you'll have them memorized before the week is up," she said.

"Maybe," I said. I scraped something yellow and sticky off one of the plates and it got stuck to my rubber glove. I flicked my hand over the garbage to try and get it to fall off. "Oh, this is so disgusting."

"What is it?" Whitney asked.

"I think it used to be eggs," I said.

"Did you ever do that project in school with the eggs?" Whitney asked.

"Once we had to design something that was supposed to protect raw eggs. Then the principal dropped them all off the roof, and whoever had an egg that didn't break won a prize," I said.

"Did you win?"

I shook my head. "I wrapped my egg in Styrofoam and duct tape, and it still smashed when it hit the ground. Is that the egg project you did?"

Whitney shook her head. "We had raw eggs too," she said. "But we had to take care of them like they were our kids."

"Like pretend to feed them and bathe them and stuff?"

"More like we weren't allowed to leave them alone, like they were babies. If we went out, we had to find a babysitter for them. In the end, most of the boys ended up with broken eggs, or they cheated and hard-boiled them."

"What about the girls?"

"Oh, we got really into it," Whitney said. "We named our eggs. I even drew a face on mine so it looked sort of like a person."

"What was your egg's name?"

"Hannah," Whitney said. "It's my favorite name. I know it's dumb, but I really liked taking care of her." I noticed that Whitney called the egg "her," like it actually was a little girl. I tried not to laugh because I knew it meant a lot to Whitney. "My sister helped me make this little bed for Hannah. It was kind of like a crib. Her husband totally made fun of us, but he was always kind of a jerk."

"That sucks," I said. I remembered hearing Whitney talk about her sister at dinner the first night at camp.

"Yeah," Whitney said. "They live in Chicago now, so I don't have to put up with him anymore. They used to live in New Jersey. Actually, I used to live with them, ever since my mom died. But Gary, my sister's husband, switched jobs, so they moved away."

"Do you live with your dad now?" I asked.

"No," she said. "He died when I was a baby. I didn't even know him. I wanted to go to Chicago with Rebecca and Gary—even though I hate Gary. I still wanted to be with Rebecca. But Gary didn't want me to go with them. He's sort of freaked out about the AIDS thing. Rebecca doesn't have it, just me. I think the new job was just an excuse to get away from me. So now I live with this other family. They sometimes take in foster kids, and the mother knew me from school because she's the guidance counselor there, so it all worked out."

I wasn't sure what to say. It was hard enough for me to move in with Dad and Meg after Mom died. That's what was weird about Camp Positive—in Highlands I was used to being the kid with the saddest life, but it was different at camp.

"Anyway," Whitney said, "my egg didn't crack. I wanted to keep it for longer than just the week, but Rebecca said it was getting rotten and would start to smell, so I had to throw it away. It was sad, because it was like throwing away my kid, and I know I might not get to have any real kids. I mean, I know it will be harder for me than it is for regular people."

"Yeah," I said.

"God, what a downer I am, huh?" Whitney asked. "I swear I didn't mean to get into all this when I started talking about the eggs."

"That's okay," I said. "I know exactly what you mean."

Whitney nodded. "So," she said, "do you have any brothers or sisters?"

"Not really. I have a dad and a stepmother, and they're having a baby, so I'll have a half sister soon. But my mom died a couple of months ago, and the baby won't even be related to my mom, so it doesn't feel like she'll be my sister."

"Sometimes I feel like Rebecca isn't my real sister," Whitney said. "We're so different because she's not infected, and she doesn't really understand what it's like. That's what I miss most about my mom. I think it would be really cool if she could come back for one day a year. I'm not asking for every day. But just one day—like maybe on my birthday every year.

It's funny because when she was alive, I thought she could be kind of annoying. She would do these things that would drive me crazy—like get mad if I didn't rinse my plate a certain way, or tell me to clean my room, or she'd say something about one of my friends and it would be all wrong. Sometimes I just wanted to get away from her." I thought about my text messages to Nicole: MOS! Whitney continued, "Now all I can think about is having her back. Even if we had just one day a year—I think about what we would do together. Probably nothing much. I would love to talk to her. I would love her to just see me."

"I sometimes wonder if my mom can see me," I said. "You know, how they say dead people can watch you from heaven, or something like that."

"I dream about my mom sometimes," Whitney said. "It feels so real, like she's visiting me or something. It's such a letdown when I wake up."

"I wish I could remember my dreams," I said.

"Yeah, well, they probably don't mean anything," Whitney said. "Rebecca thinks our parents were reincarnated. Like they're walking around now in completely different bodies. Do you believe in that?"

"I don't know," I said. I remembered Father Donaldson saying Mom was with God. But what if she wasn't with God anymore? What if she was reincarnated already? Would I ever meet her again? Would she know it was me?

"If there is such a thing as reincarnation, then I hope Gary dies and comes back as an egg. I hope he doesn't even get to grow into a chicken, because his egg gets smashed on the ground."

"Maybe he'd be a scrambled egg," I said.

"A fried egg," Whitney said.

"Or an omelet," I said.

"Oh yeah," Whitney said. "With broccoli and spinach in it. He hates eating green things."

"Sunny-side up," I said.

"Right," Whitney said. "Then you could break the yolk part and his brains would ooze out."

We stood there laughing for a few seconds. Whitney turned back to the sink and rubbed a soapy sponge along the rim of one of the plates. "Hey," I said, and she looked up again. "Do you ever wonder if it's all worth it?"

"What do you mean?"

"You know, the pills, and missing your mom, and all of that. Do you think it's worth it?"

"I don't want to die, if that's what you mean," Whitney said.

"Yeah," I said. "I guess so."

"Anyway, let's change the subject. We should sing. I know you're just pretending not to know the words. Come on." She started to sing the first line of the Camp Positive theme song. *"Whatever the weather, at Camp Positive we all come together."* I started to sing with her. I knew most of the words even though I hadn't even been trying to learn them. The parts I didn't know, I hummed.

"I knew you could do it," Whitney said. She lifted her hand from the water and gave me a soapy high five.

We finished up the dishes and went outside. Robin had made it very clear that we were not allowed to wander off by ourselves once the dishes were done. We were to join whatever activity we were signed up for. After breakfast our bunk activity was softball, so Whitney and I walked over to the baseball diamond. "God, I need a cigarette," Whitney said.

"You smoke?" I asked.

"Not really," Whitney said. "But Rebecca used to always say

she needed a cigarette. It made her feel better about things."

In the distance, Robin was waving. "Come on, you two!" she shouted. She didn't seem mad at all anymore.

"Come on," Whitney said, grabbing my hand and pulling me along.

Chapter 17

A few days later, I woke up to rain plopping down hard on the roof of the bunk, kind of like it was being thrown down. At home the rain sounded softer. I guess it was a different kind of roof.

Robin made another one of her announcements during breakfast. "Unfortunately, I can already tell this day is going to be a wash—literally," she said. She smiled at her own pun on words. I rolled my eyes at Whitney, but she kept her face straight. Even though we were all done with our week of dish duty, Whitney was still being extra careful around Robin. "We were going to try out Firebird's new zip-line course," Robin continued, "but obviously that's being rescheduled."

I heard Alexis say, "That sucks." She was the kind of person who always said exactly what she was thinking. A few other kids groaned.

"Oh, don't worry," Robin said. "We'll get another chance to try the zip lines. It wouldn't be any fun in the rain, anyway.

Today is going to be a campwide movie day. So when you finish up here, go to your bunks, change back into your pajamas. Then we'll all meet in the rec room for a movie marathon!"

Robin spoke in exclamation points more than any other person I'd ever met. It made me smile.

"What?" Whitney asked.

"Robin cracks me up," I said. "Just the way she talks. You know. She kind of sounds like a cruise director."

"Have you ever been on a cruise?" Whitney asked.

"No," I said quickly. Actually I had been on a cruise—Mom had taken me on one a couple of summers before. It was only for a few days, and our cabin was really small. But still, I was embarrassed to tell Whitney because I knew she probably hadn't been on a cruise at all. "It's just that Robin sounds the way I think I cruise director would," I explained. "I mean, can't you just imagine her saying something over a loudspeaker, like, 'We have bingo on Deck Five in ten minutes! That's bingo, in ten minutes!'"

"Yeah, I totally can," Whitney said.

I was getting used to the way Robin talked, and even the way she whistled. I was getting used to a lot of things at Camp Positive. It almost felt like things back home in Highlands weren't real anymore.

The strangest thing was that I actually thought about AIDS less at Camp Positive than I did back at Highlands, even though I was now at a camp where almost everyone had it. I guess because at camp I wasn't constantly reminded that I was different from everybody else. In a way, I wished Nicole could be there to see it—even though being around her sometimes made me think about how I was different, I still wanted her to see me the way I was now. I wasn't mean to anyone.

The rec room was in the building across from the mess hall.

It seemed kind of silly to have to race back to our bunks in the rain, change clothes, and then get wet all over again on our way to the rec room. "Why do we have to put pajamas on anyway?" I asked Whitney when we got back to our bunk.

"Oh, it's fun," she said. "It's like a big slumber party. We did it a couple of times when it rained last summer, too. Robin puts on these movies from the eighties. That was when she was a teenager, and she figures we're too young to have seen the movies from back then. It'll be great. You'll see."

I pulled off my shorts and put on my pajama pants. Then I put on a new, dry T-shirt. Dad had insisted on buying me rain boots when we went shopping before camp. I thought I'd never use them, but I put them on too, tucking my pants into the boots so they wouldn't get wet.

"Everyone ready?" Amanda called. We all were.

When we got to the rec room, it was transformed so it looked like we were actually having a sleepover. There were blankets spread out across the floor, and Robin had brought in bags of popcorn even though it wasn't even ten o'clock in the morning. "You have to have popcorn to watch movies," she explained. "Besides, it's never too early for popcorn."

Everyone from Bunk Seven sat together, except for Amanda, who went to sit with a couple of other counselors, and Alexis, who sat with Claudia. I sat on a blanket in between Whitney and Natalie. Marley was sprawled out, using one of Natalie's legs as a pillow. Kyla was behind us, braiding Natalie's hair. I remembered going to Elizabeth Arden with Lisa, and I knew Kyla would've loved it. She was really into beauty and getting made up. She painted her nails a different color every few days.

Marley twisted around to face us. "Hey, can I have some popcorn?" she asked. Whitney pitched a couple of pieces into her mouth. "This is why I like camp better than school," Marley said, after she had chewed and swallowed. "Well, this and a hundred other reasons."

"Why is that?" Whitney asked.

"You know, when it's just girls, you can lie around like this. Boys would never understand."

The lights dimmed. Whitney laid back and propped her head up with her hand so she could see the screen at the front of the room. "I know people were into the zip lines, but I'd rather do this," she told me. "Days like this make me so tired. I just want to relax."

I could hear the *plop-plop* of the rain on the roof of the rec room. It wasn't as loud as it had been earlier, but it was still there. "Me too," I said.

Robin had picked out a trilogy of movies for us—*Back to the Future Part I*, *Part II*, and *Part III*. They were from the eighties, like Whitney said. I hadn't seen them before, but I liked them because they made time seem like a place that you could travel to. I had thought about going back in time before, but it was always to a time when I was younger. Now I thought about going back in time to before I was even born. In the movies, they kept saying that if you change just one tiny thing in the past, everything might get messed up in the future. But I wished I could just climb into a time machine and get to Mom before she met Travis. I wanted to make it so everything about our lives was different.

The problem was, if Mom never met Travis, then he wouldn't have broken up with her, and Dad wouldn't have seen her crying on the street. They would never have met, and I wouldn't have been born. It's hard to try and figure out if things are meant to be the way they are, or if it would be better if you could go back and change them.

In between *Back to the Future Part II* and *Back to the Future*

Part III, we had lunch brought in, and we picnicked on the blankets. Then we went back to watching the movie. By the time *Back to the Future Part III* ended, the rain had mostly stopped, but we still hung out in the rec room for the rest of the day. Robin set out a bunch of board games. I played Jeopardy! with Whitney, Natalie, and Marley. "You want to know something really dumb?" Whitney asked as she opened the box.

"What?" I said.

"When I was little, I used to watch the game shows with my sister and her husband—you know, *Jeopardy!* and *Wheel of Fortune*. I thought the host on *Jeopardy!* was the smartest man in the world. He knew the answers to every question."

"I think the answers are given to him ahead of time," I said.

"I know that *now*," Whitney said. "But it's not like they tell you that. He just says the answers whenever the contestants get the questions wrong. He's got that perfect game-show-host voice, and it sounds like he knows exactly what he's talking about. I thought he was some kind of genius, but Gary told me I was an idiot."

"Gary's an idiot," I said.

"Yeah, whatever," Whitney said. She handed me the stack of questions. "Let's play. You can be Alex Trebek."

After we finished the games, we went to the mess hall for dinner and then headed back to the bunk. Robin came in a little while later. She didn't usually come into our bunk at night, but the rain had made the whole day different. Robin handed me a couple of envelopes—one with Dad's handwriting on the front, and one with Meg's. I had been getting mail from them every few days, but I still hadn't read any of the letters. I always stuffed the envelopes, unopened, into the corner of one of my shelves.

Robin walked over to talk to Amanda and then came back

to me. "Hey, Emmy," she said, "can you step outside with me for a minute?"

I had the feeling that I was about to be in trouble, but I didn't know why. I thought about telling her that I couldn't go outside because I was in my pajamas. But I'd been in my pajamas all day, so that wouldn't make any sense. I followed her out of the bunk. I'd taken off my rain boots, so I was barefoot, and the ground felt slick and cold, like it wasn't even summer. The screen door banged shut behind us. "I got a call from your dad today," Robin said. "Is everything okay, kiddo?"

I nodded. How would Dad know if something wasn't okay anyway? I hadn't spoken to him in almost three weeks, and I didn't even write him any letters. Besides, he was the one who sent me away. What did he care if I was okay or not? I hadn't really been thinking about Dad since I was at camp, but just hearing Robin talk about him made me angry at him and Meg all over again.

"Good," Robin said. "I thought so, but I wanted to make sure. Your dad mentioned that he hadn't gotten any letters back from you, and I know he writes you a lot. I just want you to know, I told him everything was good as far as I could see. You get along with everyone in your bunk, and you made a good friend in Whitney. I didn't tell him anything about the day you and Whitney took the canoe. I figured that was your story to tell him, if you want to."

"Okay," I said. I pressed my feet together, one on top of the other, to warm them. I pressed down hard, so even though it was warmer, it also kind of hurt.

"Are you sure everything's all right?" Robin asked. "Is there anything you want me to tell him? Or anything you want to tell me?"

"No," I said. "I'm fine."

"Good," she said. "I think you're doing really well here. I'm glad you came this summer."

Marley was sitting on Natalie's bed when I got back inside. I picked up the latest envelopes from Dad and Meg and shoved them into the corner of the shelf. "You sure get a lot of mail," Marley said.

"I guess," I said. I realized it probably wasn't a good idea to keep the letters on the shelf, where everyone could see. When Natalie and Marley got up to brush their teeth, I pulled the letters out from the corner of the shelf and opened the drawer under my bed. I didn't want the letters to be near Mom's books, but it was the best place to hide them. I pushed the books over a little bit, gently. Then I put the letters in next to them, but I made sure they didn't touch each other. I ran my finger along the bindings of Mom's books, so they were the last thing I touched before I closed the drawer.

Chapter 18

The next morning, I told Whitney I thought we should have another adventure. I didn't really want to participate in any of the camp activities that day. I couldn't explain why. I just wanted us to go off on our own. "If they do the zip lines today, let's go somewhere," I said.

"Huh?" Whitney asked.

"You know," I said. "Let's just do something, without anyone else. We could even take a canoe again, if you want." I kept my voice low so no one would overhear.

"We can't today," Whitney said.

"Please," I said. "It'll be fun, even if we get in trouble. Doing the dishes wasn't so bad anyhow. Besides, you said you weren't even that into the zip lines."

"But we have the memorial service today."

"What do you mean?"

"It's this thing we do every summer. We go up the hill and

Robin reads the names of the campers who died. Then we all release balloons."

"Oh," I said. "Well, we don't have to go, do we? I didn't even know those campers."

"I didn't know all of them either," Whitney said. "But it's not like that. You'll see."

"What time is it?"

"It's always in the afternoon, after lunch," Whitney said.

"Why don't we just go off on our own this morning then," I said. "We could take the canoe and be back in plenty of time."

Whitney shook her head. "I don't think so," she said. "It's kind of an important day to be all together."

I shrugged. "I guess," I said. I knew I wasn't going to be able to change her mind.

We had breakfast, as usual, and then we were broken up into groups for the morning activities. The day was really bright and shiny. It didn't seem like the right day for a memorial service. It looked like a postcard, with a perfect blue sky and just a couple of puffy clouds in the sky. Clouds always look so soft and comfy, kind of like pillows. It's weird to think about how they would be cold and wet if you could actually touch them.

We went back to the mess hall for lunch. Robin didn't whistle when it was time to go outside. She just cleared her throat, and we all turned to listen. "As soon as everyone finishes, we'll get going," she said. I followed the crowd outside and up the trail behind the bunks—the same wood-chip trail Tamara had taken us on for the nature walk. We got to the clearing with the wildflowers that Tamara had told us about. Joanna Wallace, Dr. Vance, and the other PAs were already there. They were holding bunches of balloons in their hands like bouquets of flowers, all different colors. We each got a balloon. Mine was pink. I felt like I did when I was a little kid at the circus, taking a balloon and holding on tight so it wouldn't float away.

People moved around so we were standing in a circle again. I glanced toward Whitney, but she was looking at Robin. "It's good to be here with friends," Robin was saying. "I know everyone we're remembering today would be happy to see that we're together."

I didn't like how people did that—said they *knew* how people would feel when really they were dead. How did Robin know they'd be happy to see we were together? Maybe they would think balloons were lame.

"It's hard for me to believe how many years we've been doing this. Every year we have wonderful friends coming back to camp, and unfortunately, every year we lose a couple of dear friends." She pulled a piece of paper out of her pocket. "These are the names of the campers we've lost since we started Camp Positive ten years ago. I'm sorry to be reading this, but I just want to make sure I'm not leaving anyone out." Her voice caught, like she was about to cry. She cleared her throat. I felt something in my throat too and I swallowed.

Robin started reading the names of kids I didn't even know. Fourteen names in all. When she finished, she folded up the paper. Then she said if there was anyone we wanted to remember for any reason, we could think of them now before we released our balloons. I knew Robin was probably thinking about her niece, and Whitney was remembering her parents. I thought about Mom, of course.

Robin said we should all let go of the balloons at the same time. "One, two, three," she said. I opened up my hand and remembered a long time ago, being at the circus with Mom. She bought me a balloon and told me to make a wish and let it go. I couldn't remember what I wished for that day, but I knew what I would wish for now. I stood and watched my pink balloon floating up with all of the others. Sometimes a couple of the balloons would get too close, and it looked like their strings were getting tangled, but then the wind would blow a little bit and they'd be untangled again.

"Look at them go," someone called out. I was pretty sure it was Joanna Wallace's voice, but I didn't look away to see. "It's like they're being pulled. They must really want them up there."

I stared up at the balloons and tried to keep track of which one was mine. They were getting smaller and smaller. I wonder how far away something has to be before you can't see it anymore. What's the exact distance that is the difference between seeing it and having it disappear?

We waited until all of the balloons were out of sight. People around the circle turned to hug each other and then we all headed back to the campgrounds. A little while later, it was time for dinner. Robin made an announcement that she had arranged for us to eat hero sandwiches. "Heroes in honor of the heroes we're remembering today."

I turned to Whitney. "No way," I said. "That has to be the worst play on words, ever."

Whitney shook her head, but I could tell she was trying not to smile.

Chapter 19

That Saturday was visiting day for Camp Firebird. Robin said the campgrounds got really crowded when the Firebird parents showed up, so we Camp Positive campers had a field trip to a place called the Game Palace. The outside was made up to look like a castle, with turrets on the top and a moat out front. We had to cross a drawbridge to get in. But inside it looked more like Chuck E. Cheese. There was an arcade and a restaurant with a big buffet. In the back there was a miniature-golf course, go-carts, and a rock wall. Robin and the other counselors were there, but they let us go off and do things on our own. I guess they figured we couldn't really get lost. I played miniature golf with Whitney, Marley, and Natalie. Marley got a hole-in-one on the last hole, and she won a little stuffed animal. Afterward, we went inside to the buffet and loaded up on food.

"I just love buffets," Natalie said. "I love all the choices, and how you can go back as much as you want."

"Me too," Marley said. "It's so much better than camp food."

"Well today they're probably serving fancy stuff for all the Firebird parents," Whitney said.

"Really?" Marley asked.

Whitney shrugged. "I don't know," she said. "They could be. You know, the Firebird parents spend all that money to send their kids to camp, so they probably suck up to them."

"Is that why they have a visiting day and we don't?" Marley asked.

"We don't need one because our camp is only six weeks, but Firebird is eight weeks long," Whitney said. "The more money you pay, the longer you can stay at camp."

"Oh," Marley said.

"I bet they're all sitting at our tables since we're not there," Natalie said.

"I wonder if they put tablecloths down to make it look nicer," Whitney said.

It was weird to think of other people sitting at our tables, but mostly I didn't care. I was just glad we didn't have a visiting day. If we did, I would've had to be with Dad and Meg all day, and be reminded that I was without Mom. I watched Natalie take a bite of a mozzarella stick, but for a second I pictured Meg sitting across from me instead. If they were serving the regular camp food, Meg would probably complain about how bad everything tasted, or else she would say it tasted so good since she was pregnant. I blinked quickly to get Meg out of my mind.

It was better this way, not having a visiting day and hanging out at the buffet at the Game Palace. I had about ten different things on my plate and I ate until I was stuffed.

"You guys," Marley said, "we should pretend it's someone's birthday so we get free dessert."

"Dessert already is free," Natalie said. "It's a buffet."

"Oh yeah," Marley said.

"I don't think I could eat anything else anyway," I said.

"Sure you could," Whitney said. "It's actually good for you to eat dessert. Sugar helps you digest things. That's why dessert was invented. I'll go get us a plate of things." She got up, and when she came back she had a plate piled with cookies and a couple of different pieces of cake. I picked up a cookie and nibbled on it. I still felt full. Whitney ate two cookies and part of a piece of cake.

A little while later, Robin whistled, which meant it was time to leave. We all got on the bus to go back to camp. I was in the back row with Whitney. We turned to look out the windows and waved our hands like crazy, trying to get the people in the cars behind us to wave back. Then Robin started singing the Camp Positive song and everyone sang along. Whitney clapped for me because I knew all the words.

That night it rained again. It was more like a misty kind of rain, so you couldn't hear it on the roof. But when the alarm went off in the morning, I got up and looked outside, and the wood on the porch was dark from being wet. Whitney was still in bed. She hated getting up in the morning. I walked over and sat down on her bed, bouncing up and down a little bit to make her get up.

"Don't do that," she said. "My head hurts a little, and my stomach."

"Sorry," I said. "Are you okay?"

"Yeah, maybe I ate too much yesterday."

"I told you sugar doesn't help digestion."

She sat up a little bit. "You're probably right," she said. "Gary's the one who told me that. He was always bugging Rebecca to buy more ice cream."

"See, you can't believe Gary," I said.

Amanda came over from her side of the room and told us

we had twenty-five more minutes to get ready. "I'm not really feeling great," Whitney said.

"Do you want to rest instead?" Amanda asked.

"Yeah," Whitney said.

"Okay, I'll let Robin and Dr. Vance know you're here," Amanda said. "I'm sure you're fine. Yesterday was a big day."

Whitney nodded.

"Should I stay and keep you company?" I asked.

"No, it's okay," Whitney said. "I'm just gonna go back to sleep." I stood up from the bed and Whitney rolled over and curled up. It made her look so small.

When we got to the mess hall, Amanda went over to talk to Robin. I knew she was telling her about Whitney. Joanna Wallace came over to our table with the morning pills. I was used to taking them in front of everyone, so it wasn't a big deal anymore. I popped them into my mouth, one at a time, and took big gulps of water so I didn't feel them going down.

I wanted to check on Whitney after breakfast, but Amanda told me Dr. Vance had gone to see her. I went to the art cabin with the rest of my bunk. I figured Whitney would feel better by lunchtime, but lunch came and went without Whitney. We headed back to the bunk in the afternoon because it was still kind of misting out, and it was too wet to do any of our usual activities. Whitney wasn't in her bed, which probably meant she was resting in Dr. Vance's office. I knew she would hate that.

"Hey, Emmy," Natalie said. "Do you want to play gin rummy with me and Marley?"

"Sure," I said. Natalie had spread out a towel between our beds, and we sat on the floor to play. The screen door opened and banged shut, and I looked over to see Robin coming toward us.

"Hey, girls," she said. "How's everyone doing?" We told her we were fine. She sat down on the edge of my bed and said she wanted to talk to everyone for a couple of minutes. Amanda, Kyla, and Alexis came over from the other side of the room. Kyla was waving a hand to dry her nails. Her hand was moving so quickly I could see streaks of color in the air, a different color for each nail.

I knew it was going to be about Whitney. I knew it even before Robin started talking. I wondered what would happen if I just got up and walked out. Would Robin still tell them, or would she come after me? Would she send Amanda to get me?

I drew my knees up to my chest, and the towel got kind of bunched up. Above my head Robin was saying that Whitney felt sick because she was having a reaction to her medication, and Dr. Vance had taken her to the hospital. "Is she going to be okay?" Marley asked. I knew what she meant, but I thought it was a stupid question. None of us were really okay.

"They're giving her fluids now and basically cleaning out her system because the medication was making her body toxic," Robin said. "As soon as she's able to leave the hospital, she's going to go back to her doctor in New Jersey, and he'll work to get her on some meds that her body can handle. But most likely, she's not going to be coming back to camp. They think she'll need to take it easy for the rest of the summer."

"Poor Whitney," Marley said. Kyla nodded. She had balled up her hands. I kept thinking about how her nails were probably still wet and now she was getting them messed up. She'd have to do them all over again.

"I'm sure Whitney would love to hear from you guys, so if you want to make cards or write letters, let me know and I'll make sure they're sent out to her," Robin said.

"Thanks, Robin," Amanda said.

Robin left a few minutes later. I was still sitting on the floor even though Natalie and Marley had gotten up. We weren't playing cards anymore. I gathered all the cards up from the towel and held the whole deck in my hands. Amanda said we should all go outside and take a walk to get some fresh air. It wasn't really raining anymore, but I didn't want to go. She came over to me and offered a hand to help me stand up, like that was the reason I was on the floor. I let her help me up, but then I sat down on my bed. "I know this is hard, Emmy," Amanda said. "It might feel better to get outside."

"No thanks," I said.

She nodded. "I understand. I guess it's okay if you stay here."

I listened to the footsteps as everyone walked outside. The front door banged shut behind them. I still had the deck of cards in my hands. I pressed against the edges as hard as I could until the whole deck popped out of my hands and exploded. The cards flew all over the floor, but I didn't care. I stood up and kicked them across the floor. I tried to kick hard enough so they would fly up in the air. I kicked one all the way to Whitney's side of the room.

Whitney's bed was just like she left it. It wasn't even made up like the rest of ours. The blanket was turned down, and there was a dent in the pillow where her head had been.

I wondered what would happen to her stuff. Someone would have to pack it up, just like we'd packed up Mom's stuff. It's so weird that when you're alive you collect all this stuff—clothes and books and photos. And then you die, and it's kind of garbage. What was the point of any of it? What was the point of going to camp and making friends and trying to have a good time if everything was always just going to end badly? It didn't make any sense.

I hadn't cried or screamed at anyone the whole time I'd been at camp. But it was like a big joke. You couldn't ever get away from AIDS, ever. You couldn't ever change anything. Real life wasn't a movie. It wasn't like *Back to the Future*, where time was a place and you could make it so things were different. I kicked at the cards again. My big toe hurt.

I bent down to rub my toe. There was the drawer under my bed, and I pulled it open. It was full of the letters from Dad and Meg, and Mom's books. I felt so stupid. I was keeping the books like they were a part of Mom. But they were just garbage too. It's not like reading them would bring her back. She didn't write them. She never even told me why they mattered so much. Besides, I wanted to see Mom—really see her. I wanted to hear her voice. I didn't want her stupid books.

I started pulling everything out of the drawer and tossing it back over my head. I didn't turn around to see where anything landed, but I could hear things hitting the floor behind me, and sometimes the frame of Natalie's bed. The letters made a soft sound, but the books hit harder.

Then there was the sound of the screen door again. Amanda must have told someone in Dr. Vance's office to check on me, but I didn't care. I didn't even turn around. I just kept pulling the books out and throwing them. Someone's hands were on my shoulders. It made it harder to throw things. I bent my head down farther so my forehead was pressed up against the rim of the drawer. My head hurt and my toe still hurt. It was so weird to feel anything when other people were dead. "It's all right, you can let it out," someone was saying. There was a buzzing in my ears so I couldn't make out the voice. The person behind me moved her hands from my shoulders and tried to hug me.

"No!" I cried, twisting around. Robin was crouched down right behind me. She fell back a little as I turned around. It was a mess—the cards, the letters, and Mom's books. I could see the cover of one of the books was torn and hanging off the binding. How could I have done that? What was wrong with me? I reached out for it, and pressed the cover back down as if pressing hard enough would seal it.

"Emmy," Robin said. She moved toward me again. I held the broken book to my chest and wrapped my arms around it. Robin wrapped her arms around me. I tried to make myself stiff, the way I did when Dad and Meg had hugged me good-bye, but Robin held me too hard. I felt like I was melting. I couldn't keep my back stiff and straight. Robin moved her hand up and down my back, up and down, for a very long time.

Finally we pulled away from each other. "Everything's ruined," I said.

"We can clean it up," Robin said. "I'll help you."

Chapter 20

When I woke up the next morning, I knew camp would be different without Whitney. It was like there had been this big hole in me ever since Mom died. Then I met Whitney, and she filled it up somehow. I got to pretend everything was okay again for a little while. Now Whitney was gone and I could feel the hole again. I knew it would be there forever, because Mom was really dead. The emptiness inside me was so huge that it was inside me and outside me at the same time, like it radiated out of my chest and there was Mom everywhere. She was everywhere and nowhere. It wasn't fair. Part of me still wanted to stomp my feet and throw things. I remembered the sound of Meg's good dishes crashing on the kitchen tile at Dad's house, and the way Mom's books sounded when they skidded across the floor in the bunk.

Then there was another sound—a real-life sound—of the alarm that sounded like a whistle going off. The rest of the bunk woke up, and I watched people starting to do the usual morning things: stretching their arms up and getting out of bed. I heard

Alexis moaning about having to wake up. Marley said something to Natalie. I swung my legs out of bed, picked up my towel, and headed into the bathroom. I took a shower and brushed my teeth. I walked back to my bed and picked out clothes to wear. I put a bathing suit on under my shorts and tank top, because Amanda said we were going to head over to the lake after breakfast. I followed everyone out to the mess hall. It was like any other day.

Robin pulled me aside at breakfast and asked me if I wanted to help her pack up Whitney's stuff. I knew she was just doing it because of what had happened the day before. She probably wanted to keep an eye on me so I wouldn't destroy anything else. We finished eating and rest of my bunk walked to the lake, but Robin and I crossed the lawn and went back to Bunk Seven. I fingered the tie to my bathing-suit top, poking out from under my shirt. It felt weird to be wearing it now, since I wasn't going swimming. I could feel the straps pulling at the back of my neck. It made me uncomfortable all over. Robin pushed open the door. Whitney's suitcase was on the floor by her bed. I stopped in the doorway and looked at it. Robin put her hand on my arm. "I asked one of the guys to bring it up from storage," she explained.

"Oh," I said.

"Well," she said, holding out her arm like she was inviting me in, "shall we get started?"

I stepped inside and we walked over to Whitney's bed. It didn't take us long to pack up everything. Robin stripped the bed and I pulled Whitney's clothes off the shelves. When Robin was done folding the sheets, she opened up the drawer under the bed and put Whitney's socks and underwear into the suitcase. The bed was bare and the shelves were empty. "This must be hard for you," Robin said. "I know Whitney is your closest friend here. I didn't want you to have to come back to the bunk with everyone else and just see it all gone."

"It's weird," I said. "It looks like she was never even here."

"But you know she was here," Robin said. "That still counts."

"I guess," I said.

"Whitney's going to be okay," Robin said. "You know that, right?"

I shook my head. "No," I said. "And you don't know that either. Everyone wants us to think that we can grow up and be normal, just like everyone else. But the truth is that no one can know that. Maybe it's not even worth it."

"What are you saying?" Robin asked. "That you should stop taking pills, and we should both stop brushing our teeth and hair, and close the windows and turn off the lights, and sit here waiting to die? After all, no one knows anything. There could be a huge earthquake tomorrow that kills us all."

"That's not what I meant," I said.

"All right then," Robin said. She got up from the floor and sat on Whitney's bare mattress, patting the space next to her so I would sit down. "Listen, kiddo, I know there's more uncertainty for you because of AIDS. But you can't just live like you're going to die, because we're all going to die someday. If you sit there and wait for it, and stop trying to have fun, and stop getting up and dressed every morning, and being with other people, and making an effort to participate in the world, then your life will be miserable and it won't be worth it. You may as well just get it over with now. Besides, it's not like it used to be, back when my niece was diagnosed. People got sick and then they died right away. There's more medication now. There's more hope. Anything is possible—I don't see why you can't grow up, get married, and have children of your own. You just have to believe you're going to live a long, healthy, wonderful life."

"What about the memorial service," I said. "You read all those names."

"Some of the kids here come from poor homes. Their families don't have health insurance, so their parents don't bring them to the doctor as often as they should. They don't monitor their medication. It's harder for them to stay well. You're lucky in a way. You know how important it is to be careful about your meds and take them on time."

"But my mom went to the doctor all the time. She did everything you're supposed to do, and she still died."

"I know," Robin said. "And what happened to her was horrible and unfair. But it doesn't mean it will happen to Whitney that way. Dr. Vance got an update from the hospital. They're trying out new drugs and Whitney's already responding well. And she's living with a wonderful family now—they love her and they're taking good care of her, so her meds will be monitored just like they should be. She's going to be back here next summer. I'm sure of it. I hope you'll decide to come back here, too."

I shrugged my shoulders, wondering if she meant that, about wanting me back, after all that I had done—taking the canoe out and making a mess of the bunk. I traced the edge of the mattress with my finger. I thought about how many other kids had slept on it before, and how many would sleep on it after. I could feel Robin looking at me, but I didn't look up at her.

"Listen, Emmy," Robin said, "what happened to your mom doesn't have to happen to you, either. From what your dad tells me, you've always responded well to the medication. You just need to stay strong and keep taking it. I'm not saying this disease is easy. It's not easy at all. And I can't explain everything that happened, except to say that life is weird."

I looked up at her. "What?"

"I'm sorry, kiddo," Robin said. "That's all I've got."

I didn't say anything. I just sat there listening to Robin breathe. In, out. In, out. She took an extra-deep breath and let it out really slowly, like Caesar's last breath. One day all the molecules would be spread out, and everyone would be breathing in a part of Robin. It didn't matter if she was gone, because energy cannot be created or destroyed. Suddenly I remembered how mad I was when Dad said he was sending me to camp. I thought if I went away, Mom wouldn't be able to find me. But now I knew it wasn't true. All those scientific things were coming together in my head. I sucked my breath in as deep as I could. It didn't matter if I was at camp. I could be breathing Mom in, no matter where I was.

When I exhaled, it felt like I was letting go of something. "I'll come back here next summer," I told Robin. "As long as you want me."

"Of course I want you, Emmy," she said. "I'm so proud of you."

We sat there for a few minutes, and then Robin said that we should zip up Whitney's suitcase because someone would be coming to pick it up. I got off the bed and kneeled on top of it. Robin zipped up the edges. She turned it on its side and rolled it to the door. She told me I could stay inside if I wanted some time to myself, but I decided to go down to the lake and meet up with the rest of my bunk. I headed outside. The sun was so bright. My flip-flops smacked against the ground as I jogged down to the lake, one foot in front of the other, faster and faster. I could see the lake through the trees. When I got to the shore, I was panting a little bit from running.

"Hey, Emmy!" Amanda called. "Come on in! You're just in time!"

I didn't ask her what I was in time for. It didn't even matter. I pulled off my shorts and took off my shirt, so I was standing in my bathing suit. I took one last deep breath in, pulling in as much air as I could. Then I let it out and ran toward the water.

Later that night, when I got back to the bunk, I pulled out the letters from Dad and Meg. I didn't stop until I had read them all.

Chapter 21

I thought about the letters even after Amanda turned out the lights and we were all supposed to go to sleep. They had both written about how much they loved me. They had told me before, of course, but back then it was like something inside me didn't want to listen. Or maybe I just didn't believe them. Now it seemed true, and also kind of amazing—especially coming from Meg. After all, Dad was my real parent, but Meg and I weren't really related, so she didn't have to be that nice after I had been so mean. But still—there were so many letters from her. And she signed them all, "Love, Meg."

In one of her letters, the one I thought about the most, she wrote about Mom's funeral. She said she knew she should have gone and she was sorry she hadn't been there for me. I was sorry about things I had done to Meg too. Maybe it would all even itself out, somehow. I wasn't sure, but part of me felt better. I turned over, closed my eyes, and finally fell asleep.

The next day I thought about writing back to Dad and

Meg—Meg had actually included stationery and stamps in her very first letter to me, so I knew she wanted me to write back. But I didn't really know how to begin. Besides, camp was ending soon and they probably wouldn't even get the letters before they saw me.

On the last day, Dad and Meg came to pick me up. It felt like so long since I'd seen them, which was strange because it also felt like it had all gone by so fast. How could time move quickly and slowly all at once? I didn't get it. It was the weirdest thing about camp—it was familiar and comfortable, and it sort of felt like I could stay there forever. But suddenly it was all over, and time to go home.

We were outside and I could see Dad's white sedan winding around on the dirt road. It disappeared again behind the trees, but I knew he was just parking the car in the lot behind the bunks. I felt like something was rising up inside me. When Dad and Meg came walking through the trees, I started running. I thought I was going to run straight into them, but when I got close, I just stopped. I was so scared, all of a sudden. It was like when I was a little kid and my grandparents would come to visit. I would be so excited to see them, but when we met them at the airport, I would hide behind Mom's legs, because part of me didn't really remember them. Then Mom would tease me for being shy.

"Emmy Lou," Dad said, stepping forward so the space was closed between us. He wrapped his arms around me. I hugged him back. "Oh," he said, sounding surprised. All of a sudden, I was crying. I held on to Dad because I didn't want anyone to see. My face was smushed up against his shoulder, and I finally let go because it was hard to breathe.

"It's good to see you, too," Dad said.

I wiped my eyes with the back of my hand, and then I turned to Meg. Her face was rounder than I remembered, and I wondered if that was part of being pregnant. It seemed weird, since the baby was in her stomach and not in her face. Her stomach was absolutely enormous. It looked like maybe there was more than one baby inside of her. When you're away from someplace, it seems like everything just stands still without you there. But I could tell things had changed. Meg held out an arm toward me, and I hugged her, but it was awkward because we had to hug around her stomach.

"I know, I'm huge," Meg said. "But we only have three weeks to go. Maybe not even. I already packed my bag for the hospital, so it's just waiting by the front door. The doctor said I could go early."

"Or you could go late," Dad said. "Emmy was born two weeks after her due date."

"Bryan, bite your tongue!" Meg scolded. "I don't want you giving this baby any crazy ideas."

Robin came over to say hello to Dad and Meg. She hugged Dad like he was her long-lost friend, even though she had met him only once, six weeks before, when I was dropped off at camp. Then she put her hands on Meg's stomach, just like Nicole had that time in my room. Part of me wanted to do it too, but I wasn't ready yet. It almost felt like Meg knew too much about me. She knew how bad I could be, how I smashed all the dishes and made her cry on the floor. It was strange because Robin was saying all these nice things about me to Dad and Meg. She said it was a pleasure to have me at camp, and that I'd promised her that I'd be back next summer.

Dad seemed to agree with everything Robin was saying, because he was nodding and smiling. "Good for you, Emmy Lou," he said.

We stood around talking for a few minutes. Meg said she had to go to the bathroom, so I took her into my bunk. She waddled across the lawn with me. It's so funny, the way pregnant women walk. It was kind of like the way Seth and Riley looked when they were first learning to walk, teetering back and forth. "Oh boy, am I ready to not be pregnant anymore," Meg told me. "I have to pee about every ten minutes. You should have seen how many times I made your dad pull into a rest stop, and you know how much he loves doing that."

"Yeah right," I said. "He thinks stopping is just wasting time." We had gotten to the bunk so I pushed open the door. Inside everything was all packed up. Meg waddled back to the bathroom and I sat on my bed and waited for her. It still felt like my bed, even though the sheets and blankets had been stripped off and packed away. It reminded me of Mom's house, with the furniture still there even though all the shelves and drawers were empty on the inside.

Meg came back out and sat next to me on the bed. "It seems like you had a good time here."

"I did," I said.

"I'm so glad," she said. "I was really worried that you wouldn't. You didn't write us back, and I thought you must hate us for sending you here—me especially, since it was my idea."

"I don't hate you," I said.

Meg nodded. "There's something I have to say to you," she said. She was sitting so close and looking right at me. Her eyes seemed to have changed colors, sort of, from clear blue to something deeper.

"What?" I asked.

"I'm sorry I didn't go to your mom's funeral."

"I know," I said. "I read your letter."

"Yes, but I need to tell you this out loud, too—not just in a letter. It was a huge mistake not to be there. It was partly because of the baby—I really had heard that it's bad luck to go to a funeral when you're pregnant. But that's an old wives' tale and a horrible excuse to have missed the most important day in your life. I told myself it was okay because I was respecting your space. You didn't even want to see your dad after your mother died. But I should have been there for you."

"It's okay."

"No, it's not. The truth is I was really scared—scared of seeing all those people who loved Simone. They wouldn't want me there. And I was scared of seeing you going through all that. It's just—it's just that I'm the type of person who tries to fix everything."

"I know," I said.

Meg smiled. "Yes, I guess you do know that about me," she said. "But of course I couldn't fix the fact that you were at your mother's funeral. I thought if I could just take care of you when it was over, that we'd all be okay. But it didn't turn out that way. It made it all even more unfixable. And we sent you to camp, and that was my fault too. You didn't write us back."

"I'm sorry about that," I said.

"No, don't be sorry," she said. "I'm sorry. I'm sorry for everything I did and didn't do. You needed to come here and figure things out, without any pressure from your dad or me."

I nodded. I felt kind of uncomfortable. Even though things were changing, it wasn't like everything was magically better. It wasn't like the movies, when you can go back in time and make it right. The worst parts were still true. But maybe things could get fixed between Meg and me. Meg patted my knee, which was the kind of thing I would've hated before I went to camp. I didn't mind so much anymore. I liked that Meg was nice to me. I wanted to be nice to her, too. I still missed Mom, and it made it impossible for things to ever feel completely right. It wouldn't ever be as perfect as it looked in the pictures. But I was going to do my best. That's what Mom would want. "Meg, can you do me a favor?"

"Of course, honey."

"Can you take me to your haircutting place when we get home?"

Meg grinned. "Absolutely," she said.

Dad came in a few minutes later to get my suitcase. There were only a couple of other kids whose parents were picking them up. Everyone else was taking the bus home. Part of me wished I were taking the bus too, just to have a couple more hours with everyone from camp. But there was another part of me that felt like I belonged with Dad and Meg. Dad went to load my stuff into the car, and I walked back out to the big lawn to say good-bye to everyone. I hugged everyone from my bunk and all the counselors and even kids I didn't get to know that well. I wasn't sad, but I still felt like crying. Robin came over and put her arm around me. "It'll be next summer before you know it," she said. "You just wait and see. Time goes so fast."

I swallowed hard. "I know," I said. I knew all about time moving fast. Time moved too fast sometimes, and you couldn't do anything to stop it. You could remember the things that happened, but you couldn't go back. You could only go forward.

"And we have our camp reunion in six months," Robin continued. "So you'll see everyone again even sooner!"

"I can't wait," I said.

Robin gave me one last hug. "Okay, kiddo," she said. "Your parents are waiting, so you better get going."

"Okay," I said. Natalie and Marley came over to walk me to the parking lot. Behind us I could hear people calling, "Bye, Emmy! Keep in touch, Emmy!" We got to the car. I hugged them good-bye and climbed into the backseat. Dad started up the engine and I twisted around so I could see Camp Positive behind me. We passed the welcome sign with the teepee.

"Arrivederci, Camp Positive," Dad said. I turned back around and faced forward.

On the way home, Dad and Meg asked me a hundred different things about camp. It was like they were catching up for all the letters I didn't write them. There was so much to tell them. We spent the whole ride just talking about camp, except for the times Meg made Dad pull into a rest station so she could go to the bathroom.

Before long, Dad made the turn off the highway that was the exit for Highlands. I knew all the roads, all the twists and turns. I started to think about Mom, because it used to be just the two of us in the car all the time. When I was little, we'd take a drive to visit a friend, and on the way back she'd let me navigate. "Make a right at the big tree. Now make a left after two stop signs." Mom would pretend that she didn't know how to get home without me. I realized it was the first time that coming home after being away a long time meant home to Dad's house, and I wasn't sure I was ready. The ride home from camp felt shorter than the ride going had been. I said that to Dad as we pulled onto our street.

"It always seems to be faster going home," he said. "The anticipation is over."

I didn't think he was right about that, because I was anticipating a lot about being home. So much had happened to me over the summer, and everything felt different. We pulled into the driveway. My heart was pounding. I pulled at the handle on the door, ready to open it.

"Hold on," Meg said. "I really have to pee, but I want us to walk into the house all together. Can you two wait out here? I'll run in and go the bathroom, and then I'll come back out, and we can just pretend we're walking into the house for the first time. Okay?"

Dad laughed. "Okay," he said. I said it was okay too, even though I didn't understand. It wasn't like this was a brand-new house and it was the first time we were going over the threshold. I let go of the handle and watched Meg through the window as she waddled as fast as she could to the front door. By the time she came back out, I didn't feel the anticipation as much. She waved to us so we knew it was okay to come out of the car. Dad popped the trunk to get my suitcase. He pulled it up the walkway, and Meg opened the door.

The sign was the first thing I saw. It was strung up across the foyer, and it said, WELCOME HOME, EMMY, in big block letters. When I got closer, I saw there were swirly designs inside the letters. It was so intricate, like a maze. I turned to Meg. "Did you do this?"

"Yeah," she said. "I'm still nesting, so I'm really into projects right now."

"It looks professional," I said. "It looks like something you could buy in a store. I mean, except for my name."

"I have software for work so I can make things like this," Meg said. "I designed it and then I brought it to the printer to have it printed out."

"Then she tried hanging it by herself," Dad said. "She pulled out the little step ladder before I even knew what she was doing. I came in here and I saw her climbing on top of it. I thought she would topple over."

"It was a team effort," Meg said.

"Thanks," I said. "It's really great. Nobody's ever made a sign like that for me before."

"I'm so glad you like it," Meg said. "We actually thought about having a few people over for dinner tonight, but we didn't want to overwhelm you. I was worried that the sign might even be too much. But everyone's been calling—your aunt and uncle,

Lisa. Nicole called this morning when we were leaving to pick you up."

"Nicole called?"

"Yup," Meg said.

"How did she know I was coming back today?"

"I saw her mother in the supermarket last weekend," Meg said. "I told her you'd call her back when we got home."

Suddenly the feeling of anticipation was back. I hadn't even had my cell phone with me at camp, and I didn't really think about anyone calling me. I headed upstairs to my room to call Nicole back. Dad said he'd bring up my suitcase in a little while.

My room was exactly the way I left it. The bookshelves were empty where I'd taken off Mom's books. I sat on my bed and picked up the phone. I still knew Nicole's number by heart, and she picked up after the first ring. "Hey," I said.

"Hey."

"It's me, Emmy."

"I know your voice," Nicole said.

"Yeah," I said. "Well, I'm home. Meg said you called."

"I did," Nicole said.

It was much more awkward than the way our phone conversations usually went. Nicole had no idea what had happened to me at camp, and I didn't know what she had done for the past six weeks. She could still be mad at me for not telling her I was going to camp in the first place. Or maybe she had decided it was too hard to be best friends with the sick girl. Maybe she had spent the summer hanging out with Rachel, Isabella, and Julia. Or maybe even Zach Andrews. She could have lots of other friends and not need me. When Mom died, it seemed like she was the only person I needed. I pushed everyone else away because all I wanted was to have her back. No one else seemed to matter. It wasn't true anymore.

"Meg said she was thinking about having a few people over for dinner tonight," I said.

"Oh," Nicole said. "She didn't tell me that when I called this morning."

"She didn't end up inviting anyone," I said. "But I don't think she'd mind if you came."

"I'll come if you want me to come."

"Of course I want you to," I said.

"Well, how do I know?" Nicole asked. "You went all the way to camp without telling me. You didn't even write."

"I know," I said. "I messed up and I'm really sorry. But I do want you to come tonight. I wouldn't have asked if I didn't want you to come."

"Okay," Nicole said. "I'll go check with my mom and call you back."

I hung up and waited for Nicole to call me back. Her picture of Brody Hudson was still hanging on the wall. Whitney said famous people liked doing things for sick kids. I had all that stationery that Meg had sent me left over from camp. Maybe I would write him a letter and ask him to send another autographed picture so Nicole could have one too. The phone rang and I picked it up. "My mom said that's fine," Nicole said. "What time should I be there?"

"Whenever you want," I said.

She came over a couple of hours later. Dad had answered the door, and I met them in the foyer. Nicole looked up at the welcome-home sign. "It looks like you're having a party," she said.

"We are," I said. "But it's a very exclusive party, so you're the only guest."

"That's right," Dad said. "No riffraff allowed."

"Cool," Nicole said.

"Meg's cooking up a storm, so I hope you're hungry," Dad said.

"I'm starving," Nicole said. "I've been running after Riley and Seth all day. I made them lunch, but Seth spilled milk all over everything, so I didn't get to eat. And then I went to clean it up, and Seth goes, 'Hey Nicole, did you know there's a paper towel that doesn't leave a streaky trail like other paper towels?'"

"Isn't that a commercial?" I asked.

"Yup," Nicole said. "The kid is reciting commercials now, but he says it in his regular voice, like it's something he made up in his own head. Wait till you hear it."

I smiled, because if she wanted me to hear Seth, that meant she was still my friend. It felt like we were sort of back to normal. There we were in Highlands, where all the bad stuff had happened, and I was okay.

Chapter 22

A week later, Dad woke me up in the middle of the night. "We have to go, Emmy," he said. He switched on the light next to the door just as I opened my eyes.

"Ow," I said, squeezing them shut again. "Why did you do that?"

"Meg's having the baby now," Dad said. "You have to get dressed."

I opened my eyes again and swung my legs out of bed. Dad left me so he could take care of Meg. I didn't know what to wear to go to the hospital. It seemed like an important thing—there was going to be a whole other person in a few hours, but it would probably look weird if I showed up at the hospital in a skirt or dress. I put on a pair of jeans and a T-shirt. Then I stood in front of the mirror, feeling sort of underdressed. "Emmy Lou!" Dad called.

"I'm coming," I said.

Dad and Meg were waiting for me by the front door. Meg

didn't really look the way I expected someone who was about to have a baby to look. I mean, she looked just the same as usual. She wasn't crying or pushing or anything like that. We went out to the car and I climbed into the backseat. Dad pulled out of the driveway. We were headed to the same hospital where Mom would go sometimes. She hated being in the hospital, and she always tried to make the doctor let her go home. But a few times she had to stay overnight. I remembered thinking the word "patient" was a good word for what Mom was. When we were there, we were always waiting. Waiting for the doctor, and waiting for her to get better. Sometimes Mom would fall asleep, and I'd sit by her bed and wait and wait for her to wake up. I always felt restless, not patient at all.

Dad turned a corner and Meg reached out and gripped his shoulder. It was something Dad told me never to do when he was driving, because it could startle him and we could end up having an accident. But he didn't get mad at Meg. "Contraction?" he asked her.

"Yeah," Meg said. Her voice came out like a whisper.

"Okay," Dad said. "I'm marking the time. Just breathe, like we practiced. Just breathe."

I could hear Meg's breaths, quick and heavy, like she was panting. After a couple of seconds, she let go of Dad. "Oh no, oh God no," she cried.

"Honey, you're great," Dad told her. "You're doing great."

"I forgot my bag," Meg said. Her voice was whiny and she sounded much younger. "I planned everything and I was so prepared, but I forgot my stupid bag."

"It's okay," Dad said.

"No it's not," Meg said. "All my stuff is in there. My clothes, the baby's clothes. It's right by the front door, but I forgot it. How come you let me forget it?"

"I was distracted," Dad said. "I can go back and get it once the baby's born. Don't worry."

"I had pills for Emmy in there," Meg said. "What if labor lasts for twenty hours? She can't miss a dose!"

"Meg, we're going to a hospital," Dad said. "We can always get pills from the pharmacy there. It'll be okay."

"It's not," Meg said. "I'm not ready. It's too early. I'm supposed to have two more weeks."

I thought Meg wanted to have the baby early. The day they picked me up from camp, she sounded like she was all ready for the baby to come out right then. I wanted to remind her, but I was kind of afraid to say anything. Meg was quiet again. Dad had one hand on the steering wheel and the other on her knee.

We got to the hospital a few minutes later. Dad pulled up right in front of the emergency room. Meg had another contraction, and Dad gripped her hand and breathed in that funny way with her. When it was over, he left us in the car and ran inside. He came back out followed by a woman in a nurse's uniform, who was pushing an empty wheelchair. Dad opened the passenger door and stepped back. The nurse leaned in toward Meg. "Hi there, I'm Gail," she said.

"Megan Price," Meg said.

"It's good to meet you, Megan," Gail said. "Do you want to walk, or do you need a ride?"

"I can walk," Meg said. She pushed herself out of the car. Dad motioned for me to get out too. He told me to stay with Meg while he parked.

I followed behind Meg and Gail. Even though I'd been to the hospital a few times with Mom, I'd never been there so late at night. Somehow I thought it would be dark on the inside, like when you wake up at home in the middle of the night. But it looked the same as it did during the day, except a little less crowded. Gail seemed to be wide awake. Maybe she always worked at night. Maybe she was nocturnal and slept during the day, like a raccoon or a bat.

We were led into a hospital room. Gail helped Meg into a gown and onto the bed. Then she strapped something around Meg's stomach that was hooked up to a machine to monitor the baby. I turned around while Gail hiked up Meg's gown to examine her. "Looks good," I heard her say. "You're at eight centimeters. Dr. Belden will be in soon."

"Thanks," Meg said.

"You can turn around now, Emmy," Gail said.

"Oh no, it's starting again," Meg said. "God, my back hurts."

Gail moved behind Meg and pressed into her back. She turned to look at the monitor. "All right, it's almost over," she said. I thought the monitor was just to see the baby's heart rate. I didn't know you could see the contractions on it.

"Okay," Meg said. "It's done."

"How far apart have the contractions been?" Gail asked.

"I don't know," Meg said. "My husband was counting. Five minutes, maybe."

"That's good," Gail said. "When Dr. Belden comes in, she may give you a shot to speed things along. In the meantime, I'm going to check on your husband and see if he got stuck filling out the paperwork. I'll be back in a few minutes, and I'll bring you some ice chips."

"Thanks," Meg said.

Gail started to walk toward the door and I got scared. What if the baby came when no one else was there? "Wait," I said.

"What?"

"It's just . . . isn't the baby coming?"

"Oh no, hon," Gail said. "It's still a couple of hours away.

You just hold down the fort for now, okay? I'll be right back."

"Okay," I said. I walked over to the monitor by Meg's bed, which was beeping. There were squiggly lines and numbers flashing on the screen. 141. 146. 139. I hoped Gail was right about the baby taking another couple of hours. I hoped Meg wouldn't have another contraction before Dad or Gail came back in.

"How does it look?" Meg asked.

"Good," I said, even though I had no idea what anything on the monitor meant.

Meg shifted in bed. I could hear the sheet rustling as she moved. "I can't believe this is happening now," she said. "I can't believe I'm about to be someone's mother. Can you believe it?"

I shrugged. "I guess so," I said. Meg had spent the past nine months nesting. It was weird that she couldn't believe it.

"And you'll be someone's sister," Meg continued.

"Yeah," I said. I stared at Meg's stomach and wondered what would happen when the baby came out. Would it go back to normal right away? It was so huge right then. Why did one little baby make her stomach so big?

Dad came in, followed by Gail and the ice chips. Meg had another contraction, and afterward they started talking about normal things, like the weather. Gail said she'd heard there was supposed to be a big storm. "But it's totally clear out," she said. "I could even see the stars when I went to meet you at the car. How do these weathermen really know when a storm is going to come? Can't the wind just change direction without warning and send the clouds the opposite way?"

"That's why you always see them predict the weather in percentages," Dad said. "They'll say there's a fifty percent chance of rain, or a seventy percent chance of rain. I've never heard them say there's a one hundred percent chance of rain."

I thought it was strange that they were talking about the weather in between Meg's contractions. There was a chair in the corner of the room, so I sat there. It felt safer. I leaned my head against the wall and closed my eyes. I wasn't sleeping, because everyone else was talking. Every few minutes, Meg would have a contraction and her breathing would change. After a while, the doctor came in to examine Meg and give her a shot. "We're almost there, Meg."

Meg called out to me and I got up and walked over to the bed. I felt like I had to hold on to something because I was so tired. Meg reached out a hand toward me and I took it. "You can stay in here if you want, when the baby comes," she said. "Your dad and I talked about it, and we decided we would leave it up to you."

"I don't know," I said. "I don't want to be in the way."

"You wouldn't be in the way," Meg said. "But you can wait in the waiting room if that makes you more comfortable. It's entirely up to you. I think it would be sort of amazing to see your little sister being born."

I didn't know what to do. Nothing gross had happened yet. But I knew when the baby came, there would probably be blood. *I'll just close my eyes,* I told myself. *I can always close my eyes.* "Okay," I said.

Meg smiled. She pulled my hand toward her stomach, which felt really hard. I had expected it to feel different, softer, like a pillow, but it was more like a blown-up basketball.

Things started to happen really fast. Meg had another contraction. The doctor came into the room. Dad and I had to leave to wash our hands and put on paper gowns and caps. We came back in, and Dad stood next to Meg. Gail was on the other side of her. I moved back toward the corner. Dr. Belden was sitting on a little stool in between Meg's legs. "All right, Meg," she said.

"Here comes another one. We're going to start pushing now."

"What do you mean 'we'?" Meg asked. "It's just *me*. I'm the only one who has to do this."

"You can do it," Dad said.

Meg sat up and made a noise that sounded like an animal. Dr. Belden was counting. "Okay, Meg," she said. "You can lie back down again." I watched Gail wipe Meg's forehead with a cloth, like Meg was a baby herself and not the one having a baby.

"I hate this," Meg said. "I really hate this."

After a few seconds, Dr. Belden said it was time for Meg to push again. Meg sat up. She was grunting and screaming at the same time. It was so loud, like she didn't care at all who heard her. I'd never heard anyone cry like that. Even when Mom was really sick, she wouldn't cry in front of me. She didn't want me to be too scared. I pressed my back up against the wall. Meg was sweating so hard that her hair looked like it was slicked back with gel.

Then, just like in the movies, Dr. Belden said, "I can see the head." I stepped just a little bit closer. They were still telling Meg to push, and Meg was crying that she couldn't.

"You're almost there," Dad said.

"Okay that's it, stop pushing," Dr. Belden said. There was a pause. Just for a second, everything was quiet. Even Meg. And then I heard the baby crying. "It's a girl," Dr. Belden said, like it was a great surprise. She held up the baby. The cord was still attached, and there was blood all over. My heart was pounding. It was like I could feel the blood pumping in my body. The baby's blood was clean and safe, but mine wasn't. Someone handed Dad a pair of scissors so he could cut the cord. Dr. Belden put the baby on Meg's chest. Dad leaned over so his face was pressed up against Meg's. They looked like a family.

After a few minutes. Gail picked up the baby and brought her over to me. There were clumps of blood and weird white globs all over, even in the little wisps of hair on her head. I shook my head and looked away. "You know," Gail said, "I once heard that when they film these things in movies, they cover the babies in cream cheese and jelly to make it look authentic. Just pretend it's cream cheese and jelly. It's not so bad."

I looked back at the baby. It was so weird. She was just there. Yesterday she wasn't, and now she was. It was like magic, the way things happened. It made me think of Mom. I thought about how her birthday was coming up. I hadn't wanted the baby to be born around Mom's birthday, but now it felt like it must mean something.

"I'll get her cleaned up now and bring her right back in," Gail said.

"Okay," I said.

"Emmy, come over here," Dad said. I walked over to the bed. Meg was still crying a little bit. There was blood on her hospital gown from where they put the baby on her chest. Dad put his arm around my shoulder. "You did great," he told me.

"I didn't do anything," I said.

"Yes, you did," he said. "You were perfect. Now you just need to decide on the name—Rose or Sadie."

"Don't tell her who picked what name," Meg said.

"Okay," Dad said. "I won't tell. Should we name her a boring, grandmother name, like Rose?"

"Bryan!" Meg said. She was laughing and crying. "Rose is a beautiful name."

"It was your grandmother's name."

"I loved my grandmother. Sadie doesn't even sound like a name for a baby."

Gail came back in with the baby. She was wrapped up in a

little white blanket with pink and blue stripes on it. I guess it's the kind the hospitals use so it works if the baby is a boy or a girl. "Do you want to hold your sister?" Dad asked me.

"Yeah," I said.

Gail handed me the baby. "Careful with her head," she said. "Just prop your arm like that. That's it."

"She's so tiny," I said. "I can't believe someone so small is actually a person."

"She's actually a little bruiser," Gail said. "Eight pounds, nine ounces."

I couldn't imagine her being any smaller. She was so light in my arms. I hoped she wouldn't break. Her eyes were closed. Being born must be exhausting. I wondered how long she would sleep. Dad leaned over my shoulder. "She looks like a Sadie, don't you think?" he asked.

"Hannah," I said, surprising myself. I hadn't even thought of that name since that day with Whitney in the kitchen of the mess hall.

"Oh, I love that name," Meg said. "Hannah Price."

"What about a middle name?" Dad asked. "We said the middle name would be whichever name Emmy didn't pick."

"I think her middle name should be Rose," Meg said. "I'm the one who actually had to push her out of my body. All eight pounds and nine ounces of her. No wonder it hurt so much."

"Hannah Rose sounds better than Hannah Sadie anyway," I said. "Sorry, Dad."

Meg reached out toward me. "Can I hold her again?" she asked. Dad picked Hannah up out of my arms. He leaned over to kiss her forehead, and then he transferred her to Meg. Hannah's eyes cracked open for an instant. They were so dark that they looked mysterious. It was like she knew a secret. Maybe it was part of the magic. She closed them again before I could even tell what color they were. Meg ran her finger along the side of Hannah's face. "I wonder what you'll grow up to be," Meg said.

"A doctor," Dad said. "A lawyer, an acrobat."

"Don't pressure her," Meg said. "You can be anything you want, honey bun."

Right then it felt like anything was possible, like nothing bad had happened. I leaned in toward Meg and the baby. "Welcome to the world, Hannah Rose," I said. *It's really weird,* I thought. *I think you're going to like it.*

Chapter 23

Dad took some time off of work after Hannah was born, and Meg's parents came to visit, so the house was really crowded. But after a couple of weeks, Dad went back to work and Meg's parents left, so it was just Meg and me in the house with the baby. We had a new routine. Hannah woke up really early, and Meg would feed her and change her. Then when I got up, I would play with Hannah while Meg took a shower. We would switch again so I could shower and get dressed. Afterward, we sat around in the den and took turns holding her. Sometimes people came over to visit. Meg made everyone wash their hands before they touched the baby.

Nicole had been away with her parents and the twins when Hannah was born. She called as soon as they got back and said she wanted to come over. She said Seth and Riley wanted to come too, but Meg said she didn't think it was a good idea because they might not be gentle enough with the baby, and they might have germs. I knew she was being overprotective, but Hannah was just so little. I didn't want anything bad to happen to her either.

I sat in the den with Meg, who was feeding Hannah. When the doorbell rang, I got up to answer it. "Make sure she washes her hands," Meg said.

"Don't worry, I know," I said.

I walked to the foyer and opened the front door, but instead of Nicole, there was a package on the front stoop. The label had Hannah's name on it. She had been receiving tons of presents. Every time she got another one, I remembered Mom's birthday—it was getting closer and closer. Of course Mom wouldn't be getting any presents this year, but sometimes I thought about what I would get her if she were alive. Maybe books, because she loved reading, or a framed picture of the two of us. I wished I had enough money to buy her a gown by her favorite designer, like one of the dresses I saw in New York with Lisa. I would bring her breakfast in bed. I would sit next to her and hold her hand and never let go.

I picked up the latest box for Hannah and brought it into the den. "Another one?" Meg asked.

"Yup," I said.

"This kid already has more stuff than I do," Meg said.

I took the letter opener from Dad's desk and ripped open the packing tape on the box. Inside was a smaller box wrapped up in pink and blue paper—wrapping paper for a baby, not for Mom. "I feel bad that people keep buying special baby wrapping paper for Hannah's presents and she's not even the one opening them," I told Meg. She was taking a break from feeding Hannah, and she had her up on her shoulder, patting her back.

"When I was young, my mom wrapped things up in newspaper," Meg said. "She would send me to birthday parties with presents wrapped up in the *New York Times*. She thought wrapping paper was a waste of money because it just got thrown away."

"I guess she was right," I said. I ripped the paper off the box. Inside was a little silver spoon engraved with Hannah's initials.

"I know," Meg said. "But I hated it anyway. I remember once being at a birthday party, and the birthday girl's mom said how pretty the bows were on every single present. Then she got to my present and she said, 'Meg's wrapping is so practical.'"

"That's embarrassing," I said.

"Tell me about it. I'm not going to put Hannah through that." She lowered her voice and rubbed her hand up and down Hannah's back. "Come on, honey bunny. Just one burp, please? Then we can finish your bottle."

"Do you want me to try?" I asked.

"Sure," Meg said.

I got up from the floor and sat down on the couch next to Meg. She handed me the baby. I put Hannah up on my shoulder, and she dropped her hand so it rested right under my chin. She always did that. Meg said she thought Hannah liked that spot because it was warm. I held her close and rubbed her back up and down, patting it gently. After a couple of minutes, she let out a loud burp. Meg and I laughed. "It's so funny how someone this cute can make a noise that sounds like that," I said.

"There's no dignity in being a baby," Meg said. "But you're like the Baby Whisperer. Do you want to give her the rest of the bottle?"

"Yeah," I said. I moved Hannah from my shoulder to my lap, propping her head up a little bit. She moved her head back and forth a little bit in the crook of my elbow, like she was getting comfy.

Meg handed me the bottle and I pushed it gently into Hannah's mouth. She started to fall asleep, so I jiggled the bottle just a little bit to wake her up and remind her to keep eating. The doorbell rang again, and Meg went to answer it. I heard voices in the hall. Meg was telling Nicole to wash her hands, and then they came into the den.

"Oh my God," Nicole said. "She's so cute."

"Yeah, we think so," Meg said.

"Can I hold her when she's done with the bottle?"

I looked up at Meg. "Of course," Meg said.

Nicole sat next to me and Hannah. "I can't believe we have to go back to school in a couple of weeks," she said. "We should just hang out here every day instead."

"I don't know what I'm going to do when you guys have to go back to school," Meg said. "I was getting so used to having Emmy around to help. I told Bryan I wanted to homeschool her, just to keep her here."

"Really?" Nicole asked.

"No, not really," Meg said. "Emmy's already smarter than I am. I wouldn't have anything to teach her. But I am going to miss her."

I was getting used to being with Meg and Hannah every day. Having a baby around was hard work, but it made things easier too. When I was with her, all I had to do was take care of her. I didn't have to worry about any of the other stuff. But things always change. Just when you get used to one routine, it's time to start another. "I'll miss you guys, too," I said.

The next day, Dad came home from work early to take me to my regular back-to-school doctor's appointment. When we got to Dr. Green's office, Gina was sitting at the front desk and she told us the doctor had an emergency and was running about an hour behind schedule. Dad said we should go to the office supply store and pick up school supplies while we waited. We got back in the car and drove over to Staples. I picked out a bunch of spiral notebooks, each with a different-colored cover.

The blue one was for English. Green was social studies. I was debating about whether to get a red or an orange one for history, when Dad came over with a package of twenty-four pencils. "I don't need that many," I said. "I only use pencils for math, and I like the click kind, not the ones you have to sharpen."

"Okay," Dad said. "I'll take these back and pick up a couple of the mechanical pencils. What about pens and highlighters?"

"I like black pens better than blue ones," I told him. "I don't really use highlighters."

"Really? What about if you're studying something, and you want to highlight something important?"

"Then I just underline it in black pen."

"Right," Dad said. "I guess that works, too."

I nodded. It was the first time I was doing the back-to-school things without Mom. I couldn't remember if she knew that black pens were my favorite. Or maybe I liked them best because they were the kind she used to use.

Dad came back with the right kind of pens and pencils. "Do you need anything else?" he asked.

"I don't think so," I said.

"All right," he said. "Let's go check out." I followed Dad to the register and he paid for everything.

"Thanks for buying everything for me," I said.

"No problem, Emmy Lou," Dad said. "I'm your dad. That's what I'm here for."

"Yeah, but at least you didn't have to pay for camp," I said.

"What do you mean?"

"Camp Positive was free, right?" I asked. "My friend Whitney said it was free for everyone."

"Technically it was," Dad said. "But Meg and I took the money we would've spent to send you to a regular camp and donated it to Camp Positive."

"Really?"

Dad nodded. "We thought it was a great program and we wanted to support it," he said. "I'm just glad you ended up liking it so much."

I thought about that day with Whitney, when we went out on the canoe and she told me everything at Camp Positive was donated. In a few months I would see Whitney at the camp reunion—I had spoken to her on the phone a couple of times. The last time we spoke was the day after Hannah came home. I called Whitney to tell her the baby's name, and she told me she was feeling better. She said she was getting ready to go back to school and planning to go back to camp next summer. But I probably wouldn't tell her about Dad giving money to the camp. I just knew that I was lucky, in a way. "That was really cool of you," I told Dad.

"Thanks," he said.

We got into the car and drove back to Dr. Green's office. Gina said I could go right into the examining room. "Room three," she said. "You know where it is, right?"

"Yeah," I said.

"Good," she said. "There's a gown in there for you, so you should just change and Dr. Green will be with you in a minute. You know the drill."

Dad sat down in the waiting room, and I walked back to the examining room. I put on the paper gown and stepped up on the scale to weigh myself. Dr. Green knocked on the door and then opened it. "Ah," he said as I stepped down from the scale. "You're doing my work for me. Thanks."

"You're welcome," I said.

I sat down so Dr. Green could take my blood pressure and listen to my heart. He checked my muscle tone and said everything looked good. Then he called one of the nurses in. I knew the blood tests were coming. It was always the worst part. The nurse came in and stretched out the tourniquet. "All right, Emmy," she said. "Which arm?"

"My left one," I said. I always picked my left arm because I was right-handed, and my arm sometimes got sore from being stuck by the needle.

She tied the tourniquet around my upper arm. "Just a little prick and then you won't feel a thing," she said. She always said that. But I could feel the blood coming out, and I could feel it every time she finished one vial and switched it for another. I kept my eyes squeezed shut so I wouldn't see anything. "Okay," she said finally. "We're all done."

I opened my eyes and saw her place the last vial of blood in a slot on the tray. They were each labeled with my name on the side. My blood was really dark. No matter how many times I saw the vials of blood, I was always surprised by how dark it looked in the tube. The nurse left the room so I could get dressed. Then Dad and I went into Dr. Green's office. He signed my papers for school and told Dad he would call in the next couple of days with my T-cell and viral count numbers.

Dad and I walked back out to the car. "Is your arm sore?" he asked.

"It's okay," I said.

"Do you need anything else while we're out?" Dad asked. I shook my head. Mom and I used to always get ice cream after I had my blood taken. It was a tradition that started up when I was really young, so I could have something to look forward to after all of the needles.

I started thinking about Mom's birthday again. I wasn't sure how to bring it up to Dad. For the longest time, I didn't want to talk to him about Mom at all. But I wanted to do something for her birthday. Dad unlocked the car door and opened it for me, like I was a famous person getting into a limo. I ducked into the car. Dad walked around to the other side and got into the driver's seat. He put the key into the ignition and started up the car. "Dad," I said.

"Emmy," he said.

"It's Mom's birthday next week."

"I know," he said. He turned the car off again and put his hand on my knee. "I know it's going to be a tough day, Emmy."

"I wasn't sure that you would remember. She wasn't your wife anymore when she died."

"Your mother and I grew apart," Dad said. "I guess we'd always looked at things differently. We had problems, even before AIDS came into our lives. And when she was diagnosed, it was just harder to get along. We fought a lot. Do you remember?"

"No, not really," I said.

"Well, we tried not to fight too much in front of you. There are things in a marriage you just don't tell your kids. You sometimes don't even tell your friends. I wasn't perfect, Emmy— neither of us was. There were so many emotions—fear, sadness, and incredible anger—we weren't angry at each other, but that's how it came out."

It was strange to think of Dad as scared and sad and angry about AIDS. I thought he didn't understand how it felt, but maybe he did. "I think that's why I was so mean after Mom died," I said. "But I don't think I was really mad at you or Meg. I mean, I know it wasn't your fault Mom died. I just hate that it happened. I miss her so much sometimes."

"I know, honey," Dad said. "And I want you to know that your mom and I really tried to make it work, but we couldn't. And finally, she asked me to leave. It wasn't easy, and maybe I shouldn't have. But it didn't mean I didn't care. It didn't mean I wanted to hurt your mom—I never wanted to do that. And we both just loved you so much. I still do, you know."

"I know," I said.

"Good," Dad said.

It was strange the way things worked out. If Mom hadn't had AIDS, then she and Dad wouldn't have had so much to fight about. Maybe they wouldn't have gotten divorced. Mom would still be alive, and the three of us would be a family. But then Dad wouldn't have met Meg, and Hannah wouldn't have been born. I couldn't imagine life without my little sister.

"I still think your mom's birthday is an important day, Emmy Lou," Dad said. "Is there anything special you want to do for it?"

"I don't know," I said. *Special* seemed like the wrong word. Birthdays were special when the person was alive, not when she was dead.

"We could go to the cemetery and bring her flowers," Dad said. "It can be just you and me if you want, if you're more comfortable with that."

Missing someone was the weirdest thing. Mom would always be gone, but sometimes she felt more gone. I was about to start eighth grade, and Mom was dead. Next year I'd be in high school. Getting older made her feel so far away. But it didn't feel right that she was in the ground. It seemed like she was somewhere way above me.

"I think we should release balloons instead," I said.

"Balloons?"

"Yeah," I said. "It was this thing we did at camp, to remember people."

"All right," Dad said. "Whatever you want."

"I want Meg and Hannah to come too. And I want to invite Lisa. Is that okay?"

Dad nodded. "I think your mother would have loved that," he said. I didn't even mind that he thought he knew what Mom would think, because I had a feeling he was right.

Chapter 24

I wanted to release balloons at sundown on Mom's birthday, but that was around the time that Hannah usually went to bed. Meg was afraid she would be fussy and cry. So we decided to do it in the afternoon, at a park just a couple of miles away from Mom's house. Dad had stayed home from work, and Lisa came in from New York City. We couldn't all fit in one car because Hannah's car seat and all the balloons took up too much room. Dad took Meg and Hannah, and I went with Lisa and the balloons. There were two white ones and three red ones. They floated around in the backseat while Lisa drove.

It felt like the car was moving in slow motion. The day seemed so big without Mom. All day long people had called me because it was Mom's birthday—Aunt Laura and Uncle Rob, my grandfather, a few of Mom's friends, Nicole and her mom. I kept thinking about Mom's last birthday, when she was alive so she could answer the phone herself. We'd been annoyed with each other that morning. I couldn't even remember why—just a stupid, ordinary mother/daughter thing. But we made up and that night we went out to dinner, just the two of us, at our favorite Italian restaurant. I had baked ziti and Mom had some kind of chicken dish—maybe Marsala or Milanese. I couldn't remember which one. It seemed so important to know what Mom had eaten for her last birthday dinner, but there was no one to ask.

"I turn on the next street, right?" Lisa said. I was supposed to be giving her directions.

"Yeah, the next one," I said. "You make a left, and then just keep going on the road until you get to the park."

"That's right," Lisa said. "I remember now. You know, I used to come here with you and your mom when you were a baby. For some reason you were afraid of the sand."

"I don't remember that," I said.

"Maybe it was the texture," Lisa said. "You didn't like scratchy things. You liked being on the grass more than in the sandbox."

We pulled into the parking lot and parked next to Dad's car. He was standing on the side with Hannah's diaper bag over his shoulder. Meg was holding Hannah. I saw her raise her hand like she was pointing to something, maybe a bird or a plane.

Lisa and I got out of the car. I opened the door to the back-seat to get the balloons. There was one for each of us, even Hannah. I gathered the ribbons in my fist and walked with everyone into the park. It was one of those parks that had everything—a baseball diamond for Little League games, a playground, a small pond with ducks in it. Dad, Meg, and Lisa followed me along the path toward the picnic area. If anyone saw us, they probably thought we were having a little party. We stepped off of the path and onto the field. I wanted to find a spot that wasn't too close to any trees. I didn't want to risk one of the balloons getting caught in the branches. "Here," I said. "This is good."

"Okay," Dad said.

I gave everyone a balloon, except for Hannah. I kept both hers and mine in my hand. I felt like I was going to cry. Dad came up behind me and put his arm over my shoulders. It was heavier than Mom's arm, or at least heavier than the way I remembered Mom's arm used to feel. But it wasn't bad.

"Should we let go all at once?" Meg asked.

"Not yet," I said. "I have to say something first." Then I stopped. "I don't know what to say."

"Do you want me to start?" Lisa asked. I nodded. She took a deep breath. "Well, Simone, it's really hard for me to believe that we're here without you. I think about you every day, and I really want to thank you for being my friend. And thank you for raising Emmy the way you did, because she is a wonderful friend of mine too."

Lisa turned to me, so I knew it was my turn. "I just really miss you, Mom," I said. I felt myself start to cry, but I swallowed and kept going. "It's been so long without you. A lot has happened and I hate that you weren't here to see it. I have a sister now—her name is Hannah. I even got to name her. And I'm going back to school next week—eighth grade, can you believe it? I'm going to start reading those books you gave me. I didn't have time to read them at camp, but I'm going to read them all, I promise, and I'll remember you forever and ever. Happy birthday, Mom. I love you."

"That was beautiful, Emmy," Meg said. I nodded, even though I knew nothing I could say would ever be enough. I wanted to describe every moment to Mom. I wanted her to be there with me.

"Are you ready now?" Dad asked.

"Yes," I said. "Now we can count to three and let them go."

"Okay," he said. We counted together and released them. The balloons floated up. I sort of felt like I was being lifted up too, just like the balloons. I kept my head tipped back and watched them get smaller and smaller. I wondered where they would end up. It was impossible to know. But they had to go somewhere. Nothing could disappear forever.

Hannah shrieked suddenly and I turned to see her. Meg was still holding her, swaying back and forth a little bit. I turned back to look at the balloons but I couldn't see them anymore. They were too far away.

"Can I hold Hannah now?" I asked Meg.

"Of course," she said. She handed her over. I put Hannah up on my shoulder. Her hand found that place under my chin and I leaned my cheek against her head.

A few minutes later, we walked back to the parking lot. I put Hannah into her car seat in Dad's car. I pulled her arms through the straps and then clicked the buckle together. Meg leaned over my shoulder. "You're a pro," she said.

"Thanks," I said.

I turned to walk to Lisa's car, because I was going to ride with her again. "See you at home," Dad said.

"Okay," I said. What a difference a few months made. Now, when I heard that word *home*, I thought of his house, not Mom's. It was so weird.

"Hey, Dad," I said. "Do you have the key to Mom's house with you?"

"Yeah, why?"

"I want to go there with Lisa," I said. Then I turned to her. "Is that all right?"

"Of course," she said. "I didn't realize you still had the key. I thought it would've sold by now."

"Actually," Dad said, "we got a bid this morning. I'm sorry, Emmy. I was going to wait until after today to tell you." Did it mean something that the bid came on Mom's birthday? Maybe she really could see me. Maybe she was trying to tell me something.

"It's okay," I said. "I just want to go there to say good-bye."

Dad nodded like he understood. He pulled his key ring out of his pocket, twisted a key off of it, and handed it to me.

I didn't have to tell Lisa how to get to Mom's house. She knew the way. When we pulled up in front of the house, it looked bigger somehow. I hadn't been there since the day Nicole and I had a fight and I walked out of school at lunchtime. The key was in my hand. I made a fist around it so I could feel the edges against my palm. Lisa and I walked to the front door. I put the key in the lock and turned to the right until I felt the little click that meant the door was open, and then I pulled the key back out.

"Are you ready?" Lisa asked.

"I think so," I said. I put my hand around the knob, thinking about how many times Mom had done the same thing. I wondered if her fingerprints were still on it. How long can fingerprints stay on something before they fade away? I turned the knob and pushed open the door. Lisa and I walked through the little front hallway to the living room. Our furniture was still there, but now that the house was sold, it would be gone soon too.

I thought of that expression, *If these walls could talk*. What would they say about Mom and me? About what it was like when we lived there? It was like I could hear an announcer's voice pointing out different things. "Here is the wall that Emerson Price drew on with a royal blue crayon. Up the stairs and to the left is the room she was sent to when she got in trouble." I followed Lisa back toward the kitchen. I could still hear the voice: "This is where Simone Price cooked dinner every night. She made Emerson set the table." I looked at Mom's chair at the table. She always kept a pillow on it to make it more comfortable. It was still there and I walked over to touch it. I looked at the way the sunlight came in through the window. In the mornings when Mom sat at the table to do her crossword puzzles, she didn't need to turn on the light. I just wanted to soak it all up—the way the chair looked with the pillow on it, the way the light came into the room—because it was probably the last time I would see the house that way, the way it looked when Mom and I lived in it, when it looked like our house. I wanted to throw my arms around it. I wished it were possible to hug space, and hold it in. I wanted to feel it, and feel her hugging me back.

Lisa and I walked around the house like we were in a museum looking at paintings. Everything that happened seemed like so long ago, almost like it had happened to another person. I could picture it in my head like a movie. The strangest thing was that whoever moved into our house wouldn't remember Mom or me at all. It would be a new house to them. It wouldn't have any memories in it.

"It's really weird here," I said. "It doesn't even feel like my house anymore."

"How is it now, living at your dad's house?"

"It's mostly okay," I said. "I didn't think it would be. I still miss Mom all the time, but it's different now." It was hard to explain out loud how it was. When Mom died, I didn't want to be close to anyone. I just wanted to be back with Mom. Part of me still expected her to come back. I knew it was stupid, but it's hard to imagine the rest of your life without the most important person you know.

"I'm always here if you need me," Lisa said.

"I know," I said. "It's getting better."

The thing is, you get better slowly. You feel better, and then for a few days you feel a little worse, and then you feel better again. Sometimes I would look at the photos of Mom and me and think about how it all used to be. But you can't ever be the way you were before. You can't ever really visit the past again, like in *Back to the Future*, because life isn't a movie. I was a different person now, without Mom.

A few minutes later, I told Lisa I was ready to leave. We locked the house up and got into the car. Lisa said she wanted to pick up a snack on the way back to Dad's house. She knew how Meg was about health food, and now that Meg wasn't pregnant anymore, she had stopped eating junk food. She was on even more of a health kick than usual, because she wanted to lose all the weight she'd gained when she was pregnant. Lisa and I went to the supermarket to get chips and ice cream. As we walked out of the car, I heard someone call my name. I looked up, but I couldn't see who it was. "Hey, Emmy, over here," the voice said.

I turned again to look behind me, and there was Aaron Bay, waving from across the parking lot. I waved back. "See you next week at school," he called out.

"See you," I said. I watched Aaron get into his mother's car and then I turned back to Lisa.

"Who's that?" she asked.

"Just this kid from school," I said.

"He looks cute," Lisa said.

"I know," I said. I didn't know what was going to happen and I still missed Mom, but I could hear her voice again in my head: *Anything is possible.*

Chapter 25

The next weekend I had to babysit for Hannah. Meg was one of those mothers who didn't like to leave the baby alone with anyone, not even me. But Dad had to bring his car in to be serviced, and he needed Meg to drive to the service center to pick him up, so Hannah and I were on our own.

She was still so little, but she was doing new things every day. It was really cool, like, every day she could have a new trick. She had started to smile, and she could hold her head up, sort of. She wasn't quite as floppy as she used to be. She had her own personality. It was so weird that someone so little was really her own person. She let everyone know what she liked and didn't like. She liked being held and rocked. She smiled the most when you were standing up and holding her. She didn't like it as much if you rocked her while you were sitting down. And she hated being put down, even if it was just for a minute. It was like she was afraid you would forget to ever pick her up again. That's when she would start to cry.

Meg left me a list of instructions, even though she and Dad would only be gone about an hour. "Don't worry about it," I told her. "I know how to take care of Hannah."

"I know you do," she said. I had Hannah in my arms, and Meg leaned in to kiss the top of her head. "The emergency numbers are in the kitchen, right by the phone."

"I know," I said. "I live here, remember?"

"Of course," she said. She hugged me and Hannah together, like she was going to be gone for a month. When she let go, I lifted up Hannah's hand and made her wave good-bye.

Finally Meg left and I brought Hannah into the den and put on some music. Meg had bought special baby CDs. At first I thought they were dumb. I mean, how could babies really tell the difference between baby music and regular music? It's not like Hannah understood any of the words. But the funny thing was that she really seemed to like the CDs Meg picked out. I swayed back and forth with her in my arms. Already she seemed so much bigger than she did when she was first born. I thought about Seth and Riley—how they could get so excited about things, they would bounce up and down and giggle. Sometimes Seth would just crack himself up for no good reason, but then the rest of us would start laughing too. I hoped Hannah would be like that. I turned the music up louder than Meg usually did. I could tell Hannah liked it because she was smiling.

After a little while, we had to take a break from dancing because I needed to take my pills. I brought Hannah into the kitchen. There was a little baby seat set up by the table, and I put Hannah into it so I could get a glass of water and my pills. Right away, Hannah's face started to crumple. "Don't worry, Hannah-banana," I said. "I'll pick you back up in a minute. Don't be scared."

I got a glass out of the cabinet and the juice out of the fridge.

I popped open the tops of my prescription bottles and counted out the pills. Hannah was crying in the background, but not too loudly. Maybe she was just testing me, to see if I would come back. I picked up the first pill, put it on my tongue, and took a gulp of juice. There were three pills in all, but I had to take them one at a time because they were so big. I swallowed another one, and Hannah started crying harder.

"Just one more pill to go," I told her. "Emmy will be right back." As soon as I said it, I remembered something about Mom. When I was little, she would sometimes talk in the third person and say things like that, *"Mommy's coming."* I had forgotten all about it. But remembering it like that, suddenly, didn't make me too sad. It was a nice thing to think about actually.

I knew I would always remember Mom, even if I wasn't concentrating on remembering her all the time. Even if the people who made a bid on her house really bought it and moved in, and painted all the walls, and planted new flowers by the walkway. I didn't need her house, and I didn't need to push Dad and Meg away. Mom would always be with me, and I would always be her daughter.

I picked up the very last pill and held it between my fingers, and then I did the weirdest thing: I kissed it before putting it on my tongue, because it was keeping me well. Life was weird, like Robin said, but it was also important. I wanted to live.

I took one last gulp of juice and swallowed the pill down. "Here I am, baby," I said as I walked back toward Hannah's baby seat. I thought about what Mom would say. Even though Hannah was crying, I could hear her as clear as ever: *I love you to the sky.*

I reached for Hannah and lifted her up, as high as I could, like I was showing her off to someone way above. It was like magic. "I love you to the sky," I said.

Author's Note

This book would never have come to be if it weren't for a woman named Elizabeth Glaser.

I was thirteen years old when I first heard about Elizabeth. It was February of 1991, and she was on the cover of *People* magazine. Under her picture, in big block letters, were the words: WHEN AIDS STRIKES A HOLLYWOOD FAMILY.

At the time, I knew a little bit about AIDS. I knew AIDS was the name of an illness caused by a virus called HIV, and that there were only three ways to contract it: from contact with infected blood, from sex with an infected partner, or from an infected mother during pregnancy or breastfeeding. I also knew you couldn't get AIDS from casual contact, which meant you couldn't get AIDS from hugging or kissing someone who was infected, or from going to the same school as someone with AIDS, or from swimming in the same pool or using the same bathroom. I wasn't scared of people with AIDS, but I had never met anyone who had it. It seemed like one of those diseases that is very sad to hear about but also very far away.

But there was something about the picture of Elizabeth on the magazine cover that looked sort of familiar to me. She was wearing gray leggings and a red sweater, and she was clutching a rock in one of her hands.

I thought she was very pretty. Her face looked serious, but also kind. I opened the magazine to read about her.

It turned out that Elizabeth was married to a man named Paul Michael Glaser. He was an actor who became very famous in the 1970s when he starred in a TV show called *Starsky & Hutch*. Elizabeth and Paul were married in 1980, and in 1981, Elizabeth gave birth to their daughter Ariel. Right after Ariel was born, Elizabeth hemorrhaged and was transfused with seven pints of blood. The blood transfusion saved Elizabeth's life, and three years later, the Glasers had another baby, a little boy named Jake.

Back then the Glaser family had the kind of life that a lot of people dream about—Elizabeth and Paul were happily married. Paul was a TV star who was directing movies, and Elizabeth loved being a mother. They lived in a beautiful house in California, just blocks from the Pacific Ocean, and Ariel and Jake were healthy and bright. But then, when Ariel was four and Jake was one, Ariel became mysteriously sick. After months of tests, the doctors realized that Ariel was sick because she had AIDS.

At the time Ariel was diagnosed, in 1986, there weren't many medications around to treat AIDS, and people with AIDS died quickly—including children. Elizabeth and Paul were terrified of losing Ariel. Their doctors told them the whole family needed to be tested as well. A few days later, there was more devastating news—Elizabeth and Jake were HIV-positive, which meant they, too, were infected with the virus that causes AIDS. It turned out that the blood transfusion Elizabeth had received to save her life had been infected with HIV. She had unknowingly passed the virus on to Ariel through her breast milk, and to Jake when she was pregnant with him. Only Paul was HIV-negative.

Right away, everything the Glasers thought they knew about life changed: Elizabeth, Ariel, and Jake all might die. They felt completely hopeless. The doctors tried to stabilize Ariel, but the disease was fairly new and the few drugs doctors had to treat AIDS weren't available for children. Elizabeth and Jake were also monitored constantly. Although they did not have full-blown AIDS, like Ariel did, they were still HIV-positive and in danger of developing AIDS at any moment. The family lived in constant fear. During this time, the Glasers' friendships changed too. People were not educated about AIDS, so they were afraid of it. Ariel had to change schools because children with AIDS weren't allowed to go to her school. The doctors told Elizabeth and Paul that they should keep the family's diagnosis a secret. They confided only in their families and a few close friends.

The Glasers did everything they could to keep Ariel well. But on August 12, 1988, two years after her diagnosis and just a week after her seventh birthday, Ariel Glaser died.

In the wake of Ariel's death, Elizabeth was determined not to lose another child. In the fall of 1988, when Jake was four years old—the exact age Ariel had been when she first became sick—Elizabeth and two of her closest friends, Susie Zeegen and Susan DeLaurentis, started an organization called the Pediatric AIDS Foundation. The foundation's mission was to raise money to funnel directly into Pediatric AIDS research, which would in turn lead to the development of more treatments for children with AIDS. The work of the Foundation provided Elizabeth with hope for Jake's future. Elizabeth also went public with her family's story and worked to raise awareness about living with HIV and AIDS. She even wrote a book called *In the Absence of Angels.*

Elizabeth's story was one of the saddest I had ever heard, but it was also one of the most hopeful. After I read the article in *People*, I bought Elizabeth's book and decided that I wanted to become involved with her foundation. I began by sending monthly donations to the Pediatric AIDS Foundation from the money I made babysitting. Even though I could afford to send only ten dollars a month, I knew I was participating in something important and making a difference in my own way.

A year later, I got to meet Elizabeth in person. I flew out to Los Angeles from New York to spend the summer volunteering at the Foundation's office. My desk was directly behind Elizabeth's, and I listened to her on the phone with doctors and politicians. Sometimes she would spin around and ask me to Xerox or fax something for her. She always hugged me good-bye when she left the office at the end of the day. I thought she was the most amazing person I had ever met, and I was completely starstruck by her.

That summer was the first time I attended the Foundation's signature benefit, "A Time for Heroes." The "heroes" at the event are celebrities who show up to support the Foundation. It was very cool to have my picture taken with some of my favorite stars, but Elizabeth was the real hero to me, and of course I had my picture taken with her as well. Later on I got to meet Paul and Jake. Elizabeth had invited me to her house for dinner a couple of days after my fifteenth birthday. She brought out a cake with Oreo frosting, and after I blew out the candles, Jake and I picked the Oreos off the top. Then we went outside to play catch on the front lawn. Elizabeth sat on the grass and watched us. She moved over to check on the flowers that had been planted next to the walkway. It was such an ordinary evening. Freckle-faced and very athletic, Jake seemed just like any other seven-year-old boy. But to me the whole evening was extraordinary, and I knew that I would always remember everything about it.

When I got home to New York, I experienced firsthand the fear of AIDS. The mother of the kids I babysat asked me not to drink out of the same glass as her children, because she knew I had spent the summer with Elizabeth Glaser and she was scared of AIDS. It seemed so ridiculous to me. How could I possibly have contracted AIDS from Elizabeth? How could I possibly pass it on to kids I babysat for? But I did as I was told and I didn't let the kids drink out of my cup anymore. At the same time I knew I had to continue my involvement with the foundation and try and educate people about AIDS. I went back to Los Angeles the next summer, and I started organizing small fund-raisers at my school to benefit the Foundation. Each time a check was sent to the Foundation, I felt a tremendous sense of pride.

The last time I saw Elizabeth was September 25, 1994. She had come to New York to attend an event benefiting the Foundation. I knew she had been ill. Susie Zeegen, Elizabeth's friend and the Foundation's cofounder, had talked to me about it. But I still didn't expect Elizabeth to be really sick; I didn't think it was possible that she would actually be dying. I was standing off to the side, watching her. She had to hold on to other people to step up to the stage. She looked so small. Elizabeth was not a tall person, but she was a few inches taller than I was, and I remember feeling much bigger than her that day.

After the speeches, someone helped her down from the stage, and she disappeared into one of the back rooms, probably to rest. I didn't see her again until the very end of the event, when people were leaving and Elizabeth came out to say good-bye. There were people all around her; some of them were crying. My heart was pounding. It was the first time that being around Elizabeth made me afraid. I walked closer. She was looking in my direction, but it seemed like she was looking through me. I wondered if she even knew who I was. She was so sick, but I really wanted her to know me. The Foundation's other cofounder, Susan DeLaurentis, had her arm around Elizabeth's shoulder. Maybe Elizabeth needed help standing. Susan saw me coming toward them. "You remember Courtney, right?" she said, and Elizabeth said yes. I tried not to cry. "I just wanted to say good-bye," I said. Elizabeth nodded. "See you next year," she told me. I remember exactly how she sounded when she said it. Her voice was so raspy. I knew it probably hurt her to speak. I stepped forward and kissed her cheek, and I remember what that felt like too, because it felt like I was kissing something very delicate, something that almost wasn't there, like I was kissing tissue paper or maybe even air.

On Saturday, December 3, 1994, Elizabeth Glaser died of AIDS. She was forty-seven years old. I keep a picture of the two of us on the bookshelf in my living room. Elizabeth is standing behind me and is gripping my shoulders. Her smile is wide and she does not look sick at all. It is the way I like to remember her. A couple of years after Elizabeth died, the foundation's name changed to bear her name: It is now the Elizabeth Glaser Pediatric AIDS Foundation.

So many years have passed since that article in *People* magazine, and a lot of things are now different in this country. There are more medications available to treat HIV and AIDS, so people are living longer lives. There are ways to block transmission from an infected mother to her baby, so fewer children are being born with HIV. The public is also more educated about the disease, so people with AIDS don't have to live in hiding.

But some things are the same. AIDS is still a very real problem in the world. Despite all the medical advances, living with AIDS is not easy. The medications can cause severe side effects, and people still die from AIDS every day. A woman I know who runs a summer camp in New Jersey for HIV-positive teens says that, despite all the medical advances, they still lose a few campers to AIDS each year. I still have the magazine from February of 1991 on the top shelf of my closet. I've kept it all this time, and when I take it out and look at the picture on the cover, I remember exactly how I felt all those years ago when I read the article for the first time: full of sadness and hope, and inspired to participate in the fight against AIDS.

Today I remain involved with the Foundation. You can't really know me without knowing something about it. My family and friends have attended benefits with me, volunteered in the office, and stuffed envelopes for mailings. Each summer, my best friend and I travel to Los Angeles to attend "A Time for Heroes."

I am also in close touch with the Glaser family. Jake Glaser is a good friend of mine. He is now twenty-four years old. Even though he has been HIV-positive since birth, he shows no signs of full-blown AIDS. He credits his mother with helping to save his life, and he often speaks at Foundation events, including "A Time for Heroes." Recently the Foundation changed the location of the event. When I walked onto the new site, Jake came over to me to say hello and asked me what I thought. "I don't know," I said. "It's not where your mother was. If she came back today, she wouldn't know where to find us."

It was a stupid thing to say; I knew it as soon as the words were out of my mouth. Jake put a hand on my shoulder and shook his head. "You know, Courtney, if I'm dealing with it, then you can deal with it." He was certainly right about that.

Every day of his life, Jake has to deal with the fact that his mother and sister are not coming back. His life has been shaped by a disease that he is still infected with. Over the last eighteen years, I have thought a lot about how I would have dealt with those life-and-death issues. And since I'm also a writer, I have written it down.

This book is about a girl named Emerson who is a lot like me: We are both sensitive and easily scared when things spin out of control. We're loyal to our friends and family but hold grudges when we get hurt. We're afraid of losing people, so we tend to cling tightly. We want things to stay the same. We can be impulsive, and we sometimes scream and throw things when we don't know what else to do. We love books and photographs. Emerson's parents divorced when she was young, just like mine did, and she has to face the confusion, anger, and sadness that come with that experience. But unlike me, Emerson is infected with the virus that causes AIDS.

Jake once said that one of the most important things his mother did was leave us with a story. Stories have the power to change your life. Elizabeth's story certainly changed mine. Although this book is a work of fiction, it is my story. I hope it is a realistic portrayal of a girl living with HIV. And I hope that it can give readers just a little bit of the understanding that Elizabeth Glaser gave to me.

Courtney Sheinmel
September 2009